M000074755

A Killer Carnival

A Provincetown Mystery

Jeannette de Beauvoir

HOMEPORT
P R E S S

A Killer Carnival: A Provincetown Mystery
Copyright © 2019 by Jeannette de Beauvoir

Published by HomePort Press
PO Box 1508
Provincetown, MA 02657
www.HomePortPress.com

ISBN   978-0-9992451-8-7
eISBN 978-0-9992451-9-4

Cover Design by Miladinka Milic

A Killer Carnival is a work of fiction. Other than those individuals who have given their permission and certain well-known landmarks, all names, characters, places, situations, and incidents are the products of the author's imagination and used fictitiously. Any other resemblance to actual events, or persons, living or dead, is purely coincidental.

Other Books
by
Jeannette de Beauvoir

Mysteries:

The Sydney Riley mystery series:
Death of a Bear
Murder at Fantasia Fair
The Deadliest Blessing

The Martine LeDuc series:
Deadly Jewels
Asylum

—

Murder Most Academic (as Alicia Stone)

Historical Fiction:

Lethal Alliances
Our Lady of the Dunes

1

By the time the float exploded, we were all far enough away that it was only ear-splittingly loud rather than lethal. I guess one has to be grateful for the small things in life. Like... well, *life*.

I don't usually spend a lot of time around objects that explode, so the experience was a new one. And in fact, there haven't been a lot of explosions in Provincetown itself, either, not since World War Two when the harbor was filled with navy vessels and the odd torpedo was taking out German U-boats right off the coast. So the float blowing up took everyone pretty much by surprise.

The fact that it was my float—well, the one I'd worked on, the one I'd had the initial idea for, the one representing my place of employment at the Race Point Inn—made its blowing up somehow even more personal.

As if someone apparently trying to kill me wasn't personal enough.

The Carnival parade starts in the East End of town, at the Harbor Hotel, and wends its way along Commercial Street as far as Franklin Street, for one long hot afternoon of total excess. P'town being P'town, a lot of the floats feature loud music and scantily clad well-oiled impossibly handsome young men dancing suggestively to a throbbing bass beat. Our float, I'd liked to think, was somewhat more subtle.

Apparently not subtle enough. Or maybe I just don't have a handle on subtlety anymore. I live in one of the least subtle places in the world, a town aggressively in your face about everything, a town with swagger to spare.

I'd like to add that, *technically* speaking, none of this was my fault. I didn't choose the summer's Carnival theme—Foreign Lands—and I didn't really mean to interpret said theme in any way offensive to anyone.

All of which is easy to say after they blow it up almost under you.

***

How is it that stories begin? "It all started when…"

… I'd gone to Orleans to have my Tarot cards read. It was two weeks before Carnival, when Provincetown goes bat-shit crazy mad and anything can happen, and I was taking advantage of a brief lull in my schedule. I'm the wedding planner for one of P'town's most prestigious inns, and summer—known here just as "the season"—is prime wedding time. But I didn't have any ceremonies that Wednesday and there weren't any fires to put out, so it felt okay to take a few hours to myself.

I know all about the buy-local concept, and there are in fact people in Provincetown who could read the cards for me, but it's not exactly like the confessional: there's no assumption of discretion, no guarantee of silence, and it's a small town. I never know what the cards might reveal, but whatever it is, I'd like to be the one to decide whom to share the results with; and, perhaps more importantly, whom *not*.

Orleans is a few towns up-Cape from Provincetown (which is actually as far out as you can get, in more ways than one), but it's a world away. The political—and, some would say, spiritual—bubble that surrounds Land's End stops somewhere in Eastham, and Orleans doesn't have quite the same spirit of *laissez-faire*. But those of us who live in P'town have that spirit, which at its best and most generous extends to accepting those outside of the bubble, too, so I wasn't looking for trouble when I stopped at the big office-supply place. We go to Orleans for things we cannot get in P'town and don't want to order online. Stationery qualifies.

I happened to be standing in a longish checkout line behind a woman wearing a headscarf—no, not just a scarf to keep the rain out, a statement headscarf that let no lock of hair escape—which was pretty unusual on the Outer Cape. I probably only thought about it myself because my boyfriend, Ali, is also Muslim. I've seen a lot of women in headscarves in Boston. There, I scarcely notice it.

The guy in front of her had noticed, and not in a good way. He kept turning around and staring at her. She kept her eyes forward, and I pretended to be interested in my felt-tipped pens. But then his buddy joined him in line, and they began a conversation that went predictably and sickeningly along the lines we in the bubble forget happen elsewhere.

"See that costume? Must be Halloween or something."

"Huh. Shouldn't be allowed in here."

"Shit, shouldn't be allowed in the country, you ask me. We send soldiers over there to defend our freedoms, and this is what we get."

This girl had to be all of thirteen years old. I looked at her face and considered the plume of testosterone in front of her and didn't know what to do.

"Hell, Jim, not our fault. She's the one wants us dead. Maybe if she'd go back where she comes from—"

"Excuse me," I said, stepping up so I was standing next to the girl in the headscarf. "Do you have a problem?"

He barely glanced at me. "You two together?"

She hadn't moved; I imagined I could actually feel her thrumming with anxiety next to me. What could I have done at that age? "Are *you* two together?"

They'd been drinking; I was realizing it now. Sydney Riley, always the last to pick up on subtle hints until they smash into her face. "Yeah, man, 'course we're together."

"Well, that's so nice to see. I hope you're very happy." I fished out a business card. "I'm Sydney Riley, from the Race Point Inn in

11

Provincetown, I'm the wedding coordinator, and we do weddings all year round. If you'd like to come and talk to me about the two of you getting married, I'd be delighted." Gotcha.

I was right. Muslim-baiting was one thing; being identified as gay was something else altogether. "Fuck, we're not together *that* way!" A register opened up then and they couldn't get away from us fast enough.

"Thank you." The girl's voice was barely audible. "I never know what to say." She glanced at me. "You know, the funny thing is, I'm from Minnesota. That's the only place I have to go back to, like they're always saying."

Well, there it was in a nutshell, wasn't it? I gave her the card I found I was still holding in my hand. "Listen, take this. My name's Sydney. I'm not Muslim, but my—partner—and his family are. I live in Provincetown. If I can ever help you, I will, you just have to call."

"Thank you." She took it and looked at me for the first time. "You're not Muslim."

I hesitated. I'm Catholic…. But. I've been rocked and alienated by the Church in so many ways, I almost admit to my religion in either a furtive or offhand way. "I've studied Islam," I said to her instead. I wasn't ready to go where my own religion might (or might not) take me.

12

The cashier called her then, and the awkwardness of the moment dissolved, and she went up to purchase her paper goods. And I stood there, belated embarrassment flooding my cheeks scarlet, wondering if I was going to go out to the parking lot and find my tires slashed. You forget, living in Provincetown, that this sort of thing happens Out In The World.

It was a small incident as incidents go. And not even particularly unique or individual; my friend Anastasia, who lives in some small town in Pennsylvania, recently had to call the police tip line to stand up for a girl working the concession stand at the movies, because some cop—in uniform, no less—was harassing her.

I thought Anastasia was brave, for talking to the police. It's easy to say, "someone should do something," but a lot harder to actually do it. I'm not always very good at confronting people who are abusive, but that doesn't mean I don't know how important it is. Otherwise we might just as well give up and go back to living in caves and being terrified of the dark.

I'm not particularly used to confrontations like that, though, and my stomach was still doing a strange little dance by the time I left and headed home. I'd expected to spend the half-hour drive contemplating the mysteries of my Tarot reading, and instead I was shaking from delayed reaction. I don't usually make a scene.

There's a line in a very old movie, the first in the Planet of the Apes franchise, in which one of the apes, played by the inimitable Roddy McDowell, is telling someone about a change of life he's experienced. "You see," he explains, "I had this accident." The person to whom he's talking (and I cannot remember who it was), says something like, "Oh, no! What happened?" And the Roddy McDowell ape says, "I collided with the truth."

I live in one of the most magical, beautiful, and tolerant places on earth. We all know the truths out there that don't always align with ours, but it's something else to have them hit you in the face. I probably should have felt empowered by standing up to a couple of bullies, and instead I was feeling small and scared, and finally I pulled into a parking lot in Eastham so I could use my mobile phone and called Mirela.

"Sunshine! I was just thinking of you. How very dynamic that you called."

I didn't try and parse the vocabulary: English isn't Mirela's first language. I think it's actually in her top five, but perfection isn't always attained; still, she speaks better than a lot of people I've heard who have only one language in their repertoire. She's an artist who came to Provincetown from Bulgaria nearly ten years ago; Provincetown liked her art and she stayed, and is now very definitely and officially a "Recognized Name." She's also my best friend. "I just wanted to hear a friendly voice," I said. I couldn't believe how much that brief encounter had me rattled. Here's the thing: I'm a wedding planner. I don't rattle easily.

"And I am friendly? Very nice. I will take it as a compliment," she said.

"Not always," I conceded. "But I can hope."

"What is wrong, sunshine?" She thinks sunshine is a term of endearment. "How can I help?"

"I just—oh, I don't know. It's too complicated to explain." Especially, perhaps, my reaction to it.

"Very good." Sometimes I fantasize Mirela learned her English by reading Wodehouse; she was in her Jeeves mode. "Do you want to have dinner with me and tell me about this complicated discouragement?"

"Actually," I said, "that sounds heavenly. But where?" It was, I should point out, August, and August is the highest of the high season in Provincetown; restaurants that take reservations are packed and all the others have lines waiting on the sidewalk. Long lines. "We could eat at the inn—" I started, but she cut me off. "We will eat at Ciro and Sal's," she said firmly.

"Okay, but—"

"Do not be tiresome, sunshine," Mirela said. "Seven o'clock. Meet me there."

"Okay." I was already feeling better. Mirela's personality doesn't so much wash over your opinions as it flattens objections like a steamroller. And it was kind of nice for someone else to take charge; that was generally my job in life, and I didn't mind relinquishing it, not one little bit.

I pulled back into the slow-moving line of traffic snaking through the towns on the way home: Eastham, Wellfleet, Truro. It's known as the Outer Cape, and Route Six takes you all the way to the ocean; next stop, Portugal. Provincetown is Land's End, and it collects the kinds of people you'd imagine would find themselves at the last stop of anything: artists, dreamers, the broken-hearted and the just plain broken. More and more, these days, it was attracting the wealthy, people who lives in their two-million-dollar condos a few weeks out of the year. There's a lot of resentment in town because of that—people who have to eat at the soup kitchen in the off-season but who must pass empty McMansions on their way there; but the truth is, they keep us alive. The summer season feeds us all year round, as tourists flock to our beaches and picturesque harbor and streets, spending their money, being a nuisance.

Me, I work at the Race Point Inn, one of the few hotels that stay open all year, and I'd be disingenuous if I scoffed too much at the visitors who enable Glenn, the inn's owner and my boss, to scrawl my name on a paycheck. Besides, I do feel a little sorry for them, even the wealthy, the ones who will earn more in a year than I will in a lifetime, because they have two precious weeks here and then they have to leave. I *live* here. I get to start every day walking on the beach. If I have to share that beach with others in the summertime, it doesn't diminish my love for this place or my enjoyment of it.

Still, times like this, on Route Six? I do rather wish they'd all disappear.

It doesn't help that there aren't any viable alternatives to Route Six. I heard a story once about a couple of guys who robbed Seamen's Bank on Shank Painter Road. Their first mistake was doing it on bicycles, which kind of tells you what level masterminds we were dealing with here. But beyond that… well, seriously, there's one road out of town. Only one. And you think they're *not* going to catch you?

Now I sat on the one road that would within an hour or so bring me back into town, and cursed my brilliant plan to spend the day in Orleans. Here's some advice: never, ever, *ever* leave Provincetown once you're there.

The worst thing of all was the cards hadn't been exactly propitious. I hoped it wasn't an indication of how the rest of the summer would go.

2

I parked my Honda—known as The Little Green Car, since in ten years of owning it I haven't been able to come up with anything more creative for a name—in my rented space up at the Monument parking lot and headed down the hill into town.

We were at the height of the insanity. Bicycles raced up and down Commercial Street, taking kids—mostly Bulgarian—from one job to another. Tourists blundered up and down as well, seeing the street as a private pedestrian thoroughfare, sometimes sauntering five or six abreast, veering off without warning to check out a shop window. It made driving to the post office something of an adventure.

The heat was wilting. We're on the ocean, sure, but Commercial Street seems to trap the heat in summer even as it allows winter winds to howl down its deserted stretches, and August feels hotter every year.

I made it to the Race Point Inn on Commercial Street in ten minutes, a new personal best for the season. I went through the main building and out to the pool, which looked enticingly blue and cool and beautiful. There were a few men in it, not swimming, just talking together, and I couldn't blame them: it looked a lot nicer than being outside. The tiki bar was doing a brisk business, too, and I wandered over to get something cold. "Hey, Tim."

He had just finished pouring something tropical with lots of fruit in it, and answered even as he slid his concoction across the bar to the customer. "Hey, Sydney, Mike was looking for you."

Mike is the inn's manager. I like him a lot, not least of all because one cold October night he'd saved my life. "Can I get a tonic with lime?" I had my priorities. "Mike say why he wanted me?"

He shook his head, spraying soda into a glass, adding ice and lime. "No. He was in a great mood, though."

"That's always good to hear. Thanks." I took the glass and held it against my forehead for a long moment before drinking. Someone in the pool said something in a snarky voice and the whole group exploded with laughter. There was music coming from one of the windows overlooking the pool. It was one of those moments you want to freeze, to make into a snapshot, to hold up and remember when the town is cold and empty and dark. What my mother used to call a Kodak Moment. I doubted anyone would get the allusion anymore.

And then the moment passed and they were just guys in a swimming pool on a hot day. I held my glass up to Tim in acknowledgment and went back into the inn. It's the most extensive in town: we have a full restaurant, two separate dining rooms, four different bars, and a spa that requires reservations three weeks in advance. You'd think with all that space I'd have an office, but you'd be wrong: what I have is a glorified cubbyhole behind the reservations desk, just out of the way of traffic going from the desk back to Mike's office.

But I love my job and I love my bosses and at the end of the day an office isn't the most important component to happiness. I checked in to see if anyone had left any notes on my desk—they hadn't—and pushed my chair in so I could get through the doorway to Mike's office. "You wanted to see me?"

He glanced up. "Hey, Sydney."

There was a sheen of sweat on his forehead. "Air conditioner not working in here?"

"Hasn't worked all week." Once upon a time not so very long ago, you didn't need an air conditioner on the Outer Cape: there were some hot days, but not unbearable ones, and the breeze off the ocean generally kept us comfortable. The past five years had put paid to that era. He shook his head. "I told Glenn we have to bite the bullet and get central air installed."

"That'll be the day." I slid into one of his visitor's chairs. "Could be worse. I just spent a couple of hours on the Route Six parking lot."

"At least you have air in the car," he growled, then flipped the ledger he'd been writing in shut. "Okay. So where are we with the float?"

The Thursday of Carnival week is the Carnival parade. This isn't exactly Macy's or the Rose Bowl: the "floats" tend to be a lot less extravagant and a lot more homemade, and music is of the club sort rather than from a marching band, but it's a not-to-be-missed part of a not-to-be-missed week, and people come from all over the Cape to crowd the street and watch. That's in addition to the thousands of people who come from all over the country to enjoy the whole of Carnival week. It's a wonder, really, the town isn't so weighted down it just sinks into the bay. The business guild chooses a theme every year, and there's a Grand Marshal and prizes, but for most people it's an excuse to get hammered and—in some instances—more than a little raunchy.

Past themes included everything from outer space to myths and legends, from jungle fantasies to the wild wild west (the leather boys had especially embraced the latter, and believe me when I say they don't leave much to the imagination), and we at the Race Point Inn usually had a float entered, at least since I'd been there. We'd even managed to squeak out a trophy now and again. Our float started out with just decorations on Mike's pickup truck, until Glenn decided to get a real base, so it really did look like a float. It was fun, and the staff always ran out of the inn to cheer it as it inched by on Commercial Street.

This year's theme was Foreign Lands, which has about a million interpretations, and Glenn the inn's owner had given me carte blanche to do something special.

"I still think," I said to Mike, "with a theme like that, it's just begging for problems. People are going to go for stereotypes, you know they are."

"Probably," he agreed. "Take it up with the PBG. What've *we* got?"

"We're using the same base we used last year," I reported. "Somebody kept it in a shed somewhere in Wellfleet. And we're doing a whole bunch of papier-mâché figures of monuments—the Eiffel Tower, the Taj Mahal, the clock tower in London."

"Big Ben."

"The clock is called Big Ben," I corrected. "The tower isn't Big Ben. It's the Elizabeth Tower." I'm really good at trivia.

He flapped a hand. "Whatever." I decided not to tell him that technically even Big Ben isn't Big Ben. "Who's on it?"

"Glenn's in the truck pulling it," I said. Glenn liked to be part of things—but not necessarily out in the hot sun itself. He's a bear of a man—in more ways than one—and sweats easily. I was surprised he hadn't embraced Mike's idea of central air conditioning at the inn. "And Clark and Gus and Evan on the float looking sexy. At least so far. We'll proba- bly get more people interested before Carnival starts."

24

"You got those papier-mâché figures done? Where are they?"

"Basement." There are warrens of cellar spaces under the inn, itself having one of the largest footprints of any place in town: wine cellars, storage cellars, a drive-in garage storing Glenn's precious red 1961 Volvo P1800, and more rooms than I could count. We were assembling the float down there: it offered more space than anywhere else, we could leave projects half-finished, and there was a modicum of cool, being underground. We're actually pretty fortunate to have any basement space at all: the Outer Cape is quite literally a sandbar, and "Cape cellars" tend to be circular and very small. Sometimes the water table rises, and they flood. Never a dull moment.

"You need any help?"

I stared at him and started to smile. "Wait, Mike—you think I'm actually down there every night working on them myself?" I am notoriously bad at anything involving crafts of any kind, which is why I have a healthy list of artisans to help with wedding decorations. If decorating were up to me, our very pretty arbor would stay naked for every ceremony. "You wouldn't want to see what I'd come up with. I've got people."

"On payroll?"

"Volunteer," I assured him. Fiscally responsible, that's our Mike.

"Good." He managed to work up a little enthusiasm. "Sounds good, Sydney. I don't think you have to worry about stereotypes, those are tourist destinations, it's like us and the Pilgrim Monument."

"Don't get me started," I told him darkly. Most people don't realize the pilgrims first landed in Provincetown, not Plymouth. Plymouth just had a better public relations agency, that's all. The Mayflower Compact was written in Provincetown Harbor, Dorothy Bradford drowned here (did she jump, or was she pushed? who knows?), and the first contact with native peoples was here. The settlers found us too inhospitable and pushed off to found Plymouth, but not before stealing food from the Wampanoag and leaving them with a few diseases against which they had no immunity. For all this we got a monument (oddly enough, modeled after a tower in Italy) to the memory of the pilgrims, who were anything but kind.

I left the pilgrims alone and went back to the float. "So what *we're* doing isn't bad," I said. "But who knows what everyone else is going to come up with? The Orient, with Charlie Chan lookalikes? Maybe a harem from Arabia?"

Mike was clearly exasperated. "Harems are made up of women," he said. "This is P'town. Don't look for problems where there aren't any." And it was true: as a primarily gay resort town, most of the skin being shown during any Carnival parade was male. I wondered briefly if any gay emirs had kept male harems. Probably.

"Okay." I knew just how far I could push him. But I was still disturbed by what had happened in Orleans, by the girl in the head-scarf and the troglodytes in the flannel shirts. "It's just—we talk about diversity, and respect, and all that, and I really hope we show it at the parade." Last-ditch attempt at an argument.

"Go away, Sydney."

I went.

***

The window air conditioner in my apartment was just about keeping pace with the heat. I opened the freezer when I got home and stuck my head in for a few moments of imaginary relief. Ibsen seemed to find that curious and let me know he was waiting for some kitty treats: get your head out of the damned freezer and take care of me.

The light was flashing on my landline. I don't really know why I keep a landline anymore; it got bundled with my cable and wi-fi and I never bothered to unbundle. Only a few people ever use it. And it's nice to have a number that works when I've forgotten to charge my mobile, which happens more often than I'd like to admit.

The first message was from Ali. "Hey, sweetheart, just have a minute here before a meeting. I'll call again later. I wanted to confirm coming down for Carnival, and let you know there's just one change—Karen's taking the week off, too, and didn't realize I had plans. I asked if she wanted to come with me, and you know it was pro forma, of course she was going to say no, I thought maybe she'd be going to see our folks, but she said yes. I'm as surprised as you are. So, anyway, if you can find a room for her somewhere, that would be great, and we can talk more later. Love you."

I stared at the machine. Ali's sister Karen is Boston's police commissioner, and the last time she'd taken a vacation had been—well, I couldn't actually remember when it had been. When she went to Lebanon a few years ago, probably. She was what my mother would have called married to her job, which sounds terrible; but in fact even if it's so, it's a happy marriage. Karen loves what she does and she does it well. She worked hard, harder than anyone I can even imagine, to rise through the ranks of a police department that's still more male than female, and she did it wearing the headscarf that marks her as Muslim. Pretty damned impressive.

We're not what I'd call close, but that's circumstantial, and I think given a chance we could really like each other. I completely and unabashedly admire her. Don't get me wrong; I'm happy with my life, but sometimes I catch myself wondering if I should have gone to graduate school or volunteered abroad or done something else meaningful on a grander scale. Weddings are meaningful, sure, but I look at people like Karen and feel a little in awe. She's changing the world. She's keeping a whole city safe. That's pretty damned impressive.

The unfortunate result of my admiration (and, let's be honest, insecurity) is that I tend to get a little tongue-tied when I'm around Karen. I mean, let's compare our days: I herded a bridal party, she whipped into a telephone booth and put on a red cape. One way or another, she's saved lives, kept people save, improved their quality of life, promoted women's issues, and fought Islamophobia. That's Karen. I think of her as just slightly lower in the pantheon than a goddess. And how do you have a casual conversation with a goddess?

Karen had been lukewarm about her religion until a while back when she spent some time with extended family in the Middle East, and came back much more observant than when she left. Ali fretted over it for a while, but she didn't seem to mind that he hadn't followed suit. Would she have preferred him to have a Muslim girlfriend? Absolutely, no doubt; but you don't get to be police commissioner without being a realist, and "as long as Ali is happy…" I don't know if she actually ever said that, but I'm sure the thought's there.

It felt eerie, being reminded twice in one day of women and headscarves. The girl at Staples, and now thinking about Karen, just seemed very coincidental. Which it was, of course; television detectives are always saying they don't believe in coincidence, but it does exist, that's why there's a word for it.

It didn't explain the sudden shiver up my spine, either.

Maybe it was the air conditioning. I picked Ibsen up for a quick cuddle, but he wasn't having any of it, so I got a cold drink from the refrigerator instead and sat down to sort my mail and maybe even my thoughts. Karen coming to Provincetown for a visit at almost any other time of the year would have been fabulous; but I couldn't see myself showing her the sights during Carnival week. Not that Carnival wasn't a sight in itself.

It was all too complex to deal with on a hot day. Anything was too complex to deal with on a hot day.

***

The story is Ciro & Sal's was originally opened to keep struggling artist Salvatore Del Deo in paints. He and Ciriaco Cozzi had met in Provincetown in the forties as students of the famed Henry Hensche, and since neither of them had any money, they opened what was then an after-hours joint where you could get cheap eats and talk all night about... well, anything. The art colony loved it. The fishing community loved it.

It's evolved into something different, and hasn't served cheap eats in decades, but what it does serve is some of the best northern Italian food on the Cape. Mirela loves it and goes there often—it's only about a block from her studio—which explains how she could snag us a table *sans* reservation.

She was already there when I arrived, sitting with her elbows on the table, studying her phone. Which is about the only thing you really *can* read in there—Ciro & Sal's goes for ambience, and everything is candles and low lighting.

She looked up when I arrived, her eyes sparkling from whatever she'd just read. Probably a review of her work. Mirela isn't just good; she's on her way to becoming one of Provincetown's greats. Hell, the century's greats. "Hello, sunshine," she said. "I ordered a bottle of wine."

I took my seat and looked around. "Probably a good start," I said.

Her eyebrows lifted gracefully. "You really *have* had a bad day," she observed.

The waiter, tall, handsome, and Bulgarian, arrived at that moment with a bottle of Chianti—not one of the straw-enclosed ones they use for décor, but something decidedly upscale. "This is Iskren," Mirela said to me, waving in his direction as he opened the bottle. He smiled and nodded and I did the same and waited while Mirela tasted, which then unleashed a torrent of Bulgarian between them. He poured both our glasses and asked about the menu in English. She was ready for him: "Carciofi alla Romanelli to start." Her Italian pronunciation was impeccable.

"And then?"

There was another spurt of Bulgarian, Mirela asking questions and Iskren presumably giving answers.

"What did you order?" I asked when he was gone.

"Artichoke hearts with other things," she said absently and raised her glass. "To a better tomorrow, sunshine." We clicked glasses and I took a very long, very grateful swallow. The wine was, of course, amazing.

"What else?" I hadn't looked at the menu. "I usually get the lemon fish."

"Iskren says the rosemary chicken is perfect tonight," she said. "So that is what I ordered. Stop being difficult, and relax, Sydney. There are more important things to think about than the menu."

That was true enough. I took another good swallow of the Chianti.

"So tell me what this is, sunshine, that has your underpants in a knot," she said, regarding me over the rim of her glass. The wine looked like liquid rubies in the candlelight. It should have been a mellow moment.

"I won't even begin to correct your imagery, though it's striking for sure," I said. I put down my own glass with a thud. "Oh, Mirela, maybe it's nothing, but everything seems so out of control. Or maybe it's just me who is."

"Define *everything*."

I took a deep breath. "So the first thing is Karen is coming down for Carnival. You know, Ali's sister."

"I know who Karen is." She nodded. "She has not been here before, I think."

"No. Yes. Okay. Well, you tell me whether it's the best of all possible ideas. She's so Muslim she makes *Ali* uncomfortable, for heaven's sake, and he's not exactly unobservant, he's someone who hasn't touched alcohol since college. Or maybe before that. Maybe never." I wondered how it was I didn't know which. I should have known. "And she's coming to P'town. For *Carnival*."

She sipped her wine and kept watching me. "She might be uncomfortable," she said, and shrugged.

"You *think*?"

Irony is lost on Mirela. "I think you are worried about something that has nothing to do with you," she said. "She will come, she might be uncomfortable, she will leave. She is not a child. She is an adult and a very intelligent and competent one. If she is coming, she knows what she is going to see. That is all. It is not your problem to solve."

Our appetizer arrived, Iskren giving us each a small plate and thoughtfully pouring more wine before leaving again. "I suppose you and Ali already have talked about this," I said. Mirela and Ali are possibly even closer friends than Mirela and me. Sometimes I was grateful for their friendship. Sometimes it drove me crazy.

She shook her head. "Not yet," she said. "Perhaps he wished to give you the good news first." She cut the artichoke and put half on her plate. "Listen, sunshine, it is not the end of the world. Karen is not an idiot. Do not treat her like an innocent, or like a child. She could eat you for breakfast, or shoot you perhaps. She is not your responsibility."

I finally tried the appetizer. It was good. "Maybe." I breathed deeply for probably the first time all day. "It's just—the whole Muslim thing's been on my mind today." And I told her about what had happened at Staples.

"We do not have a large Muslim population, here on Cape Cod," Mirela allowed, swirling her wine pensively. "Is there even a mosque?"

I shook my head. "Closest one's in Boston." And it wasn't even in Boston proper. "That's what I mean. We say we're all about diversity, but it's not a real diversity, is it?"

"It is not our fault that there is no mosque here," she said. "Diversity can mean many different things in different places. What is your point, sunshine?"

"I don't know. I don't have a point." I was feeling frustrated and dangerously close to tears. I didn't even really know what I was so upset about, the emotion was overwhelming the thoughts. "I just think if we're going to talk about inclusivity—"

She reached across the table and took my hand. "Sydney. Stop," she said.

I nodded, staring at my plate, the tears pushing their way down my cheeks. Lecturing wasn't doing anything but getting me more upset. "That girl," I said. "At Staples... if I hadn't been there..."

She squeezed my hand. "But you were. You were there."

I looked up at her. "It hurts my heart, Mirela."

"I know," she said.

"And now Karen's coming, and it's not just she's going to freak out, of course she isn't, it's that... I don't want something bad to happen to *her*. I don't want her to be treated like that. And it won't happen in P'town, of course, but I don't like it happening to anyone, of course I wouldn't, but Ali's *sister*..."

Iskren appeared with the chicken, interrupting my train of thought, such as it was. He and Mirela exchanged some words, and I took advantage of the time to dab at my eyes. With Ciro and Sal's nice cloth napkin, smearing mascara across it. I hoped they had a decent laundry service.

When he'd left, she gazed at me impassively. "What *you* need is a vacation," she said.

"Yeah, right. In August." I managed a shaky laugh. "That could happen."

"Arrange it now for the fall," she counseled. "Thinking about it, planning it, the anticipation will help."

"Okay." I pushed the chicken around on my plate.

"I mean it." She took a swallow of wine. "Sunshine, I think this is not why you are upset."

"Really? I'm pretty sure it's why I'm upset. At least I've done a good job of convincing myself."

"It is Ali," she said. "Listen to me. This is really and truly about you and Ali. You are starting to see the fissures between your world and his."

Fissures? *Fissures?* "I really didn't come here for analysis," I said, finally taking a bite of chicken. Iskren had been right: it was melt-in-your-mouth perfect. I swallowed and touched the napkin to my lips. Not the part with the mascara on it. "I just wanted to tell you about it. I just wanted to vent." I paused. "Besides, I've always been aware of the—what did you call them, fissures?—between Ali and me. For heaven's sake, he worked for ICE when we met."

"He still works for ICE now." She was looking amused.

I shook my head. "Not going after immigrants," I said. "Not that way." Ali had transferred into human trafficking not long after the summer we'd met, when my beloved friend and boss Barry had been murdered. Ali had come to town to arrest him for facilitating a marriage-for-green-card scam.

Which he hadn't been doing, anyway.

Ali had already been questioning his career choice when we met, and it hadn't all been on me to persuade him to join the good guys; he was ready for a change. At least that's what I told myself on the long nights when he was away doing something potentially dangerous. There may be *better* ways to spend your time than pursuing impoverished homeless people whose lives were so awful they'd risk everything to go somewhere else; but it turned out it was a lot *safer* to be going after immigrants than what he was doing now. The ethics and the danger seemed to line up together. "Anyway,"

I added, "we know we have differences. Every couple has some differences."

"Not always on religion," she said gently.

"It hasn't come up," I said. And it hadn't, not really: Ali was Muslim, and I was Catholic, but neither of us was particularly practicing. I went to Mass sporadically, and probably couldn't say a rosary all the way through if my life depended on it. (Um, how many mysteries are there, again?) Ali observed as far as alcohol was concerned, but didn't go to any mosque, and certainly didn't carry a prayer rug around with him and face Mecca five times a day or anything like that. Our mutuality was in our lukewarm approach to our respective faiths.

"And now," said Mirela, "you are afraid it will. You are choosing to attack rather than admit it is what you fear."

"What do I fear?"

"That he will become too Muslim for you. That there is a part of you not comfortable with it. His sister is more devout. This girl at the store in Orleans today, she is more devout. You do not know how you feel about it, and you are acting out anger you feel toward yourself on others."

I stared at her. "Do you really think so?"

Mirela shrugged. "What do I know? I am not a psychologist, me. But this is what I see. And now, we will enjoy dinner."

But I wondered with a detached part of my brain if she might be right. And how I would feel about myself if she were.

3

Ali called, naturally, just as I was getting home. "You're a hard woman to reach, Sydney Riley."

"'Tis the season," I said automatically. It's the same excuse I use with my mother, too. He generally takes it better than she does.

"You okay?"

I thought of several flippant answers and bit them all back. One of my new year's resolutions back in January had been to work on my sarcasm. As in eliminating it.

Yeah, like *that* was going to happen.

I think I was born sarcastic; or maybe it was living with my mother for my formative

years that did it. It's amazing Ali ever even
wanted to date me in the beginning, when you
consider what he put up with; I hadn't been
very nice to him at all. There must be other
women out there who are lower maintenance.
"I'm fine," I said.

"When women say they're fine in that
voice, they're not."

"What voice?"

"You know the voice. I know the voice.
Let's cut to the chase. What's going on,
Sydney?"

I sighed and flopped down on my sofa.
"It's too hot to breathe, I have a million
weddings, Carnival's coming, and oh, did I
mention, so is your sister."

There was a slight pause. "Ah. I thought
Karen might be it," he said, almost diffidently.
"That's why I told you on voicemail. So you
could get used to the idea first, before we had a
chance to talk about it."

"And not react all over you, is that what
you mean?" The wine from dinner—we'd
ended up with two bottles, after all—was
turning nasty on me. *Breathe, Riley, just breathe.* It
felt like this was all somehow Ali's fault—or at
least it ought to be.

There was a pause. "Maybe we should be
having this conversation in person."

"God, I hate it when you're so reasonable," I said. Ibsen jumped up and sniffed my hand, hoping I might have a treat or two on me. I never did. He always hoped. Some relationships are built on less.

"I don't think I've ever been in an argument where I was accused of being too reasonable," he said. There was a hint of amusement in his voice, just enough to send me straight over the edge. "Ali, what the hell are you thinking, Karen and Provincetown and Carnival all in the same week?"

"It wasn't precisely my idea," he pointed out. "What exactly did you want me to do, Sydney? Tell her she can't come, like it's a treat she doesn't deserve?"

"That might have been a good start," I said, and took a deep breath. I hate it when I hear myself going off the rails. "You know I have a million and a half things to do at Carnival," I said, trying to sound like an adult. "And I'll just get... intimidated."

"*Intimidated?* Why would Karen want to intimidate you?"

"She wouldn't. I mean, she wouldn't want to. She just does. By being herself. And I'll have to be on my best behavior and not mess up around her." I was exaggerating, of course. Too much alcohol makes me do stuff like that.

Push against the boundaries. Sabotage everything around me. So much for being an adult.

"You're saying you don't want my sister to come because she'll make you *uncomfortable?*"

"Not just me. Carnival, Ali. Scantily dressed men. And she won't wear her uniform, but she has a *presence*—"

"You think people are going to assume she's a cop? Is that really what this is about?"

Of course it wasn't. It was about my own insecurities, and not being ready to make myself and my home vulnerable. Not without a little more advance notice.

I didn't say anything. He sighed, sounding impatient. "Sydney, she'll be fine. You'll be fine. All the scantily dressed men will be fine. It's Provincetown. It's not like she needs your protection. It's not like she's going to be in some random place where people have never seen anyone different from themselves. Hell, in P'town, *everyone* is different."

"Not many Muslims, though," I said.

"What is your point?"

"Hate crimes against Muslims were up forty-three percent last year. That's not—"

"You think I don't know about hate crime statistics?" I'd finally gotten under his skin. I wondered if it was what I'd been trying for all along. "You think I don't know about anti-

Muslim sentiment? You think people don't look at me on the subway and get just a little scared? No, wait, listen, you think I'm not automatically making adjustments throughout my day for keeping white people around me from freaking out?" He paused. I didn't say anything. I could feel him taking a deep breath, and when he spoke again, he was calmer. "You never even *heard* of white privilege until you were in college, Sydney. Don't lecture me on racism."

He was right, and I was drunk. It wasn't a happy combination. "Ali, I just—"

"You know what?" he said suddenly. "She won't come. I won't come. You're making it clear you don't want us. Go sleep it off. Whatever's going on for you today, whatever this is, deal with it. I'm not arguing with you anymore."

"Ali—" But he had already gone.

I looked at Ibsen. "I think there's just an infinitesimal chance," I told him, "that I'm turning into a real bitch."

And on that happy note, I went to bed.

***

The next day arrived, as days invariably do, welcome or not. I started mine with a cracking headache and an enormous sense of guilt. Ibsen was particularly strident; he always is when I need it least. I somehow doubt it's accidental.

Somehow in the night I'd reached a couple of conclusions. One was that I had to make it up with Ali, not just because he was right and I was wrong, but also—and far more important-ly—because I loved him. And, by extension, his sister. I'd turned a tricky situation into a mountain of problems, and only because I was feeling edgy and had too much to drink.

The other conclusion was that the only way to face fears is to—well, *face* them, squarely and with as much preparation as possible. We still had a week and a half to go before Carnival, time to re-engineer some things. Like the inn's float. Making sure there was something on it to stand for Islam. Making sure it was *inclusive*. It was probably the direction my subconscious had been leading me in anyway.

But first, coffee. Gallons of it.

I showered, dressed, took aspirin and drank as much strong coffee as I could man-age. Ibsen got fed. The bed got made. Life was, apparently, going to keep going in more or less the same direction it had been heading previ-ously.

The thing was, I told myself as I set off for the inn and work, not to become racist in my attempt to educate others away from racism. My float could end up being stereotypical as hell and I'd be defeating my own purpose. I didn't want the twenty-first century equivalent of blackface or Charlie Chan, only with Middle Easterners instead. No cultural appropriation. I had to be subtle.

Yeah, right, Riley. On a *float*. In a *parade*.

But first I had some fences to mend. I started with the inn's manager. The good news was his window air-conditioner was finally working. The bad news was it didn't seem to have improved his mood. Mike was sitting at his desk, scowling at something on his laptop. He glanced up for a mere second. "Did I say come in? I'm only asking because I was listening pretty hard, and I didn't hear myself say come in." He paused. "Nope, I'm pretty sure I didn't say come in."

"I come bearing gifts," I said. I'd stopped off in the kitchen, where Angus, our pastry chef, was just starting to think about the dessert menu for tonight, and had snagged one of his options, something flaky and smelling of everyone's grandmother's dream kitchen. I put it in front of Mike, now, as a peace offering. "I was a bitch yesterday, and I've come to say I'm sorry."

He was slightly mollified, though whether at my apology or Angus' pastry, it was hard to tell. "It's hot, everyone's short-tempered," he said reasonably.

I flopped into the client chair. "You talk to Glenn about the central air?"

"About eight times. He'll hear me eventually." He bit into the flakiness and confectioner's sugar dusted his olive-drab shirt.

"I don't remember a summer this hot."

"No one remembers a summer this hot. The *dinosaurs* wouldn't remember a summer this hot. Took mankind to fuck things up this much."

I toyed in passing with the idea of correcting "mankind" to "humanity" and explaining why, then dropped it. What I didn't need to do was any more lecturing. "I want to take the float in a different direction," I told Mike.

"Yeah? What direction? As far as I'm concerned, the way I'm feeling right now, you can take it directly out to sea."

"I want to do something about all religions getting along, all people getting along. A world-peace kind of thing."

"Yeah?" he asked again, then finished off the pastry, put the plate down, and located a tissue with which to wipe his mouth. "Thought we were doing airplanes, travel, something like that."

"Let Cape Air do airplanes," I said, flipping the idea away with a hand gesture. "Let's be positive. Let's make a statement. Let's show everyone the country's current administration's wrong, the president's wrong, we don't have to live in fear and mistrust."

"And you think you can communicate all that on a float?"

"I haven't drilled down into the details yet," I said. "Inspiration will come."

He shrugged. "Sounds fine to me, long as you don't go over budget. Run it by Glenn first."

"Glenn will say yes."

4

I left Ali voicemail. I figured, depending on how angry he was, it would probably take two or three messages before he was ready to respond. If I were being honest with myself, it would have taken me even longer if he'd been as obnoxious to me as I'd been to him. I ended it with our traditional, "I love you, I love you, I love you." There's a poem somewhere he'd studied in school that said, "What I tell you three times is true." Yeah, he's romantic enough to remember it—and incorporate it into something silly and personal. And of course I think of things like that when I'm afraid I might have screwed things up.

It left me with a feeling of disconnection, of floating between options, and not liking any of them. Whether I wanted to admit it or not, Ali had become a touchstone of sanity in my life. When I panicked—and I am way prone to panic—just talking to him was enough to calm me down, to help me get perspective, to give me an overwhelming feeling of peace and that Things Would Work Out. Without it, I felt vulnerable and more than a little scared.

But there wasn't really time. I had a wedding at four-thirty, and hadn't made sure my ducks were in a row, and my experience is you always pay the price when your ducks aren't properly aligned. And some of them can be very, very headstrong. I headed back to the kitchen.

The kitchen at the Race Point Inn is a cavernous affair, mostly because Adrienne, our diva chef, has decreed it so. She is both amazing and terrifying, and she's one of the reasons people come from everywhere—and I mean everywhere—to stay and eat here. The inn has a restaurant as well as the two dining rooms for guests, and it's Adrienne who really keeps the place going all year-round: even in the coldest of winters, people come to stay and eat in the restaurant. She's that good.

She's also intensely difficult to work with, and I couldn't blame Angus, the pastry chef, for requiring his own space, his own appliances, his own everything. Not crossing paths with Adrienne is the easiest way to get along with her.

Tucked into a corner, discreetly, one of the sous-chefs was working on my wedding spread. Adrienne created the dishes; the sous-chefs executed them. "Hey, Philip."

He glanced up from the terrine he was decorating. "Sydney, doll, can't kiss you, my hands are full."

"So I see." I hitched myself up to sit on one of the pristine steel counters. Adrienne would have been after me with a cleaver if she'd seen me. "So what's up? Everything good for this afternoon?"

"How could it not be, with *moi* in charge?" He grinned, stepping back to contemplate his work. "Perfection," he pronounced, "has been attained."

"This couple's picky," I warned him. I'd had no less than twenty conversations with the two grooms over the past couple of weeks. The fact that they hadn't been in agreement on all the details hadn't helped.

"Picky," said Philip, "is my middle name."

"True enough," I agreed. "Else you wouldn't be able to work for Adrienne."

He made a moue of distaste. "Doll, there are divas who are divas in a *good* way. Cher comes to mind. Liza. Judy, for that matter. And then there's Adrienne." When he wasn't in the kitchen, Philip had a drag persona, recreating an almost-believable Cher over at the Crown & Anchor. He fervently believed every problem could be solved by asking, "What would Cher do?"

Me, I didn't really care what Cher would do, but to each their own. "She's not in today?"

"The bitch goddess? Doll, it's Monday. She's never in on Monday. Except when she wants to check up on us mere mortals." He wrapped the terrine lightly in tin foil and slid it into a refrigerator, pulling out some vegetables at the same time. "And is that why you're here? Checking up? Or do you want to make yourself useful?"

"I never want to make myself useful." I slid off the counter. "What do you need?"

"Garnish, doll. It's all about garnish."

I shook my head. "Then count me right out. I can't do all those fiddly things." Philip was in fact a culinary artist: he created roses from radishes, fountains from carrots, spirals from zucchini. The only thing I could do with vegetables, besides cook them, was stuff celery stalks with peanut butter. Not precisely what my grooms were looking forward to.

It could have been worse. My mother used to fill her stalks with some sort of cream cheese concoction, add raisins, and tell me they were bugs on a log. And that was supposed to entice me to eat them.

I will never understand my mother.

"No, not that," Philip said now, pulling out cutting boards and unwrapping his personal knife set. "Just chop some things. Nothing fancy. If you really want to help." He slanted me a look.

"Of course I do," I said heartily. Of course I didn't. But I like making sure we all play well together here at the inn, and besides, right now the kitchen was cool and echoing; I liked it that way. Angus's area was hot from the ovens, but over here it was still clean and the appliances were cold to the touch. I washed my hands and turned to Philip. "What can I do?"

He set me up with a cutting board and some carrots. "Wash them, peel them, chop them," he instructed.

I got started. "So what would you think," I said by way of conversation, "to helping with the Carnival float? We're doing peace, love, and understanding."

"Oh, doll, how Disney-esque!" Second only to Cher, Philip loves Disney. He loves the princesses. If he didn't do Cher, he'd probably figure out how to look like Snow White or Cinderella.

"I thought of it more as like the sixties," I said, peeling a carrot. I can do one for every eight or nine Philip does. Good work takes time. "You know, make love not war, peace out, all that."

"No, no," he said, and started singing. "It's a small world after all, it's a small world after all..."

"I get the idea."

"...it's a small world after all, it's a small, small world." He finished and grinned. "Pure Disney, doll."

"Maybe." Actually, now that he said it—or more precisely sang it—it wasn't a bad idea. I chose a knife at random and started chopping. We could be the antithesis to the parade's theme of "foreign lands" by saying there *are* no foreign lands. Seen from Disney, of course. Brotherhood of man or whatever the gender-equal expression would be. "You want to be on the float?"

"In less than two weeks? Gimme a break, doll. I couldn't manage a persona in that amount of time."

I half-turned to him. "I just thought maybe—" The knife slipped and sliced not carrot but flesh, the back of my left hand. Blood spurted out. "Philip!"

"Oh, shit." He grabbed a towel and my wrist at almost the same time, wrapping it tightly around my hand. "Shit, shit, shit." His eyes were on my face. "You look pale. Come on, doll, sit down, let's see what's going on here."

I was only too happy to sink into the chair. It hadn't hurt at first, but now suddenly the pain was there, fierce and sharp. Philip knelt on the floor and gently unwrapped the towel, checking out my hand. I didn't look. There are some things you don't need to see. Philip's worked in kitchens all his adult life; he's probably seen worse.

"Well, I've seen worse," he said cheerfully, mind-melding with my thought. "But you need stitches, doll, and that's a fact." He wrapped the towel back around me and stood up. "Come on. I'll take you to Outer Cape."

"But the vegetables..."

"Blood isn't my favorite ingredient," he said. "I'm keeping you well away from it."

Seeing my expression, he lost the levity. "Don't worry, doll. We'll take the Volvo and I'll come right back and get the garnishes made, you'll see, everything will be fine. You can call Mike when you're done and he can pick you up."

I was feeling distinctly light-headed, more from the thought of blood than the loss of it. "Okay."

The inn owns a couple of vehicles, mainly used for transporting guests to and from the ferry or the airport. The Volvo was ancient and in remarkable shape and bore the inn's crest on its side. Philip grabbed the keys from the front desk and got me ensconced in the front seat. "Mike could do this," I protested.

"My kitchen, my injury."

"Don't let Adrienne hear you calling it your kitchen."

Outer Cape Health Services is where we go for everything. It has an impressive list of specialty services, and is the first stop for urgent care. Anything the clinic can't handle goes via ambulance to Cape Cod Hospital, which is all the way in Hyannis and, in the summer, at least an hour and a half away, even with lights and sirens. I was very much hoping I wouldn't be sent there. There was no way I'd be back in time for the wedding.

Philip came in with me and waited while they checked me in and I sat down in the waiting room. "I'm off, doll. You have your phone?"

"In my pocket," I said, nodding. "Thanks, Philip."

"I'll go take care of that big, bad knife then," he said with a wink. "Good luck."

I sat and watched the overhead television, as I clearly couldn't manage a magazine at the moment. The woman next to me was watching, too. "Can you believe that shit?"

"What? I wasn't paying attention."

She nodded at the screen. "That god-damned group, says gays are going to hell," she said. "They're in Boston. I thought we were safe from that shit."

I nodded. Eastern Massachusetts, despite the Commonwealth's odd habit of electing Republican governors curiously frequently, is very educated and very liberal. We don't go much in for hate speech. "What are they protesting?"

"Who knows. Finding more people to hate, though. Now they're getting on the anti-immigrant bandwagon. That guy running for sheriff is saying the same thing. Saying immigrants are all terrorists." She shook her head. "I moved here to be safe from that shit."

I started to say something, but then the inner door opened and a man in scrubs called, "Sydney Riley?"

I managed to get up and cross the room, still ridiculously clutching my towel. "Hi, Sydney. Hear you cut yourself." He led the way back to an examination room.

"It was a big knife," I said, half-defensively, half-humorously.

There was a glint of amusement in his eyes. "I'm sure it was. Date of birth?"

No matter what you're there for, you go through the same routine. Meds you're on (none). Weight (are you *kidding* me? This is relevant *how*?). Blood pressure (you seriously expect it to be normal with blood seeping through my towel?). "Okay, good. I'm going to just take a quick look." I didn't want to do the same, and studied a chart on the wall talking about HIV infection and the new pre-exposure prophylaxis that was going to end AIDS within a generation. PrEP. I hadn't heard of it before. "All right, Sydney, we're going to clean this up and probably give you a few stitches. You've missed your radial artery."

"That's good, right?"

"That's very good. I'm going to leave you for a minute, and I'll be back to clean it, and

Dr. Madison will be in to see you in just a few minutes."

I'd never heard of a Dr. Madison, but I knew Outer Cape offers summer residencies to doctors—along with a cottage somewhere in Truro—as reinforcements to supplement the regular clinic staff during the busy summer season.

The nurse left and I went back to learning about PrEP. You'd have to take it daily for the rest of your life if you were having unprotected sex with relative strangers, but it seemed a small price to pay. In the 1980s, men came to Provincetown to die; there was a funeral every week. Defeating the plague seemed a good thing.

They came in together, the nurse holding a tray with things I didn't want to know about, and a black woman about my own age, with luxurious locks held up and back with a brightly patterned scarf; she had something sparkly woven into the locks. "Hi, I'm Thea Madison. Sydney, is that right? Jeremy says you cut yourself?"

I held up my hand. "Chopping carrots," I said.

"Uh-huh." She sat on a stool and scooted it over to me, taking my left arm in her hand

and unwinding the towel. "This looks like it was pretty clean," she remarked.

"We'll fire the laundry service if it wasn't," I said. "It's from the Race Point Inn."

"Uh-huh," she said again. She was focused on my hand, gently exploring the cut. I looked back at the HIV chart. For heaven's sake, I've been around people who were *shot*, so where was this sudden squeamishness coming from? "This looks good, Sydney. I think we're just going to clean it and give you a few little sutures. Are you experiencing pain?"

"Some," I admitted.

"Ibuprofen," she said. "That will help. When was your last tetanus shot?"

I had no idea. "I have no idea," I said.

The nurse was looking at the laptop. "Three years ago," he reported.

"Good, then you won't need one today. Jeremy, can you clean this while I get the stitches ready?"

They traded places and he started doing things to my hand, holding it over a basin and putting something cold on it. I kept looking away. *Breathe, Riley, just breathe.* It would be really embarrassing to pass out at this point. More for something to focus on rather than out of any real interest, I asked her, "So are you one of the summer residents?"

The quicksilver smile. "Oh, gosh, no. I've lived here two months already."

"Sorry. I didn't know," I said. "I usually see Dr. Shay."

The smile broadened. "You mean Provincetown's Favorite Doctor?" She made it sound like a title, as if all the words were capitalized. "Sorry, I'm what you get today."

"I didn't mean it like that—"

"I know you didn't," she assured me. "Okay, let's take a look at this now. Nice." She turned back to something she was fiddling with on the counter. "My partner and I moved to P'town fulltime just two months ago ourselves," she said. "We'd just met, in Boston, and I was lucky they needed a new practitioner here. I honestly wasn't sure what else I'd have done. Found something up-Cape, maybe, and then had to commute."

"That was brave, moving here first," I commented.

"The whole thing was daring," she said and laughed. "We met, we fell in love, and Emma—that's my partner's name—was determined we should move to P'town right away. That's either daring or insane."

"A little of each," said Jeremy.

"Why did you want to live here?"

"Why does anybody?" she asked rhetorically. "It's a beautiful place, it's a safe place, it's an accepting place. I didn't actually know much about Provincetown—I came here once for a Women of Color Weekend, about five years ago—but Emma was set on it. It's odd, because she really didn't know anybody here, but it's what she wanted. And, besides—I haven't talked to her about it yet, but I'd like to have children, and I'd like them to grow up in a healthy space."

I nodded. "We live in a beautiful bubble in Provincetown."

"Maybe there's no getting away from hatred these days, but we can only try. Okay, let's see your hand. I'm just going to give you a topical anesthetic here, so it doesn't hurt as much."

I appreciated that little bit at the end, the "as much." Okay, yes, I was starting to hyperventilate a little. *Slow down, Riley, breathe deeply.* "You really only met a few months ago? I asked, anxious to keep the conversation—any conversation—going, so I didn't have to think about a needle going into my skin. "That really is… brave."

She was starting the stitches now; my hand felt like it was on fire. I looked desperately at the PrEP chart. "Or insane," she said.

"Right." I was gritting my teeth. Sydney Riley, medical coward. How long did it take to put in stitches, anyway?

"All set." She rolled her stool back and Jeremy the nurse moved the tray away. "First time you've had sutures?"

"Does it show that much?"

She smiled. "You're lucky. The first time I ever got them, I was at the emergency room at a teaching hospital. I got someone who'd never done it before. I was her practice case. She thought it was fascinating. I didn't."

I managed a weak smile. "I'm glad you have experience."

"I have that, for sure." She put out her hand to shake mine. "Nice to meet you, Sydney. You can make a follow-up appointment with Dr. Shay if you want, but those stitches are going to dissolve on their own. Jeremy's going to cover that up and give you some instructions."

"Thanks." I took her hand. "Nice to meet you, Dr. Madison."

"Oh, it's Thea, please. Have a good day."

After a start like that, it had no direction to go but up.

***

As soon as I got back to the inn, I checked in on Philip, who was relieved to see me upright and apparently none the worse for wear. Angus had appeared with the wedding cake, and it was Angus outdoing himself: the couple on the top tier was *dancing*. Actually moving. He does divine French pastries, Angus does, but over the past year he's been inspired by some former graffiti artist who creates cakes with parts that move, and so Angus has been producing birthday cakes with trucks that dump jellybeans or others with Cirque du Soleil-like recreations, and wedding cakes that include ringing bells and couples scaling the sides of the cake. Next to those, I suppose the waltz here was pretty tame. "It's gorgeous," I said.

Angus nodded, satisfied. He was itching to get back to his lab. I knew he was working on something "really different" for our Carnival party next week. I wished him well.

The bower out beyond the pool and the tiki bar was all set, too: the florist was busily covering it in white and purple flowers. The champagne was chilled. The officiant, Vernon Porter—or "Lady Di" if he was *in persona*—was presumably planning to be on time. Life was under control, and it was only one o'clock.

I stayed outside, sitting on the patio swing, and called Ali again. Again I got his voicemail. "I'm actually calling to apologize," I said. "I really am sorry. I was in a bad mood and I took it out on you and the truth is I'd really, really like you and Karen to both come to Carnival next week. I have a room reserved for her here at the inn and—well, I'm sorry, is all. Okay. Call me. Bye. Wait, don't call at four o'clock, I have a wedding. Okay. Bye. I love you. Bye." I never know how to end voicemails. I end up saying good-bye about eighteen times, one way or another.

I sat there for a while, idly moving the swing and watching the florists working without really seeing them. The phone rang and I grabbed it out of my lap, not even looking at the Caller ID. "Ali!"

"No," said a voice dipped in acid. "Well. I should have *known* you'd be disappointed to hear from me instead of *him*."

My mother. And here I'd thought the day couldn't get much worse. "Hey, Ma."

"And what am I supposed to think, you're expecting a call from him but you don't have time to call me and let me know you're alive?"

That was, even for my mother, an impressive sentence. "It's nothing, Ma. We had an argument is all. It'll blow over. How are you? How's Dad?"

I know my efforts to derail her conversational goals are invariably going to fail, but I always try anyway. It's a little dance we do. "We're fine, as you'd know if you ever got in touch."

I fell back on my old reliable excuse. "It's the season," I said. "I have a wedding today. I have a wedding tomorrow. I have Carnival next week."

"But you have time to talk to *him*," she said.

My mother can't quite assimilate my relationship with Ali. My parents live in an extremely wealthy community in New Hampshire that's very white bread—well, it's white-bread as long as the bread's a baguette or a brioche. They have *standards*.

But that's not even the real problem. The real problem is my mother believes it's her God-given fundamental right to choose my future husband. She doesn't want Ali around mostly, truth be told, because she hadn't presented him to me as an option. I sighed. "Ma, do you want to talk, or do you want to fight?"

"Well, you haven't shown any interest in our health lately, but I should tell you your father's going in for a *hip replacement*." She made it sound like dangerous exploratory brain surgery. "It's going to upset the whole schedule."

Schedule? What schedule? My father's retired. My mother never worked outside the house, unless you count all the volunteer committees and clubs and organizations she haunts—um, sorry, is *involved* with. (For that matter, she hasn't done much work *inside* the house, either, to which years of professional cleaners and laundry trucks attest.) "He'll feel much better afterward," I said heartily. "Those operations are routine, these days."

"Well, it will stop him complaining all the time, anyway," she said. My mother, God bless her, can always perceive her glass as half-full, even if it's the wrong liquid in it. How he hasn't divorced her by now is a total mystery. "And he won't be able to play golf for weeks," she added.

"And that's a problem?"

"Oh, don't be ridiculous, Sydney, of course it is. He'll be underfoot all the time. It's going to be incredibly annoying. I don't know what I'm supposed to do with him around all day, complaining. I wish he'd consulted me about this whole thing. The scheduling, I mean. It surely could have been done in the winter, when there's no golf. This is all so irritating."

If there's a tsunami in the Philippines, a wildfire in California, a natural disaster anywhere on earth, my mother will find a way to make it all about her. "You'll live through it," I predicted.

"Well, of course I can't expect you to understand," she said impatiently. "The point is, it would be nice if you could come up for Sunday dinner while he's recuperating. Show some interest in your family. Help out a little, even, if it's not too much to ask."

Yeah, actually, it *is* too much to ask. Besides, I didn't know exactly what "help out" might mean to my mother. "Ma, what part of the season don't you understand? I can't come up for Sunday dinner, any other kind of dinner, until the summer's over." And, with a little luck, not then.

She treated me to a long, martyred sigh. "I suppose I should have known," she said.

"Yes," I agreed. We meant totally different things. That was okay. "Tell Dad I hope it goes well."

"You could tell him yourself if you ever bothered to call."

Times like this, I really, really hope I was adopted.

5

The planets aligned, the stars twinkled happily in their far-flung universes, and the wedding went off without a hitch. Angus' cake precipitated a gasp from the guests, something I'd never heard at a wedding before. It would, no doubt, go right to his head, and I could foresee a lot more novelty cakes with intricate moving parts in our future. The string quartet from Cape Symphony performed beautifully, Vernon Porter in full Lady Di regalia (think: your grandmother on a good day) officiated a touching ceremony, the grooms' mothers wept discreetly, and we managed not to run out of Veuve Cliquot. All in all, a rousing success.

One down, the rest of the season to go.

I left them all getting ready for their evening out on the town and hopped up on a seat at the tiki bar by the pool. Carole was polishing glasses. "Good wedding?" she inquired.

"The best," I said. "Angus' cake didn't explode." I had no idea how prescient I was being.

"You want a glass of wine?" The staff know my preferences as well as my moods.

I glanced at my watch. Six o'clock, the sun was well over the yardarm. "Why not?"

A voice behind me said, "And a ginger ale, too, please." Ali.

I gasped. "I've been trying to call you!"

He smiled, put an arm around my shoulders, and kissed me. Ali is heart-stoppingly beautiful, with his olive complexion and black curly hair. This year he was trying out some designer stubble, the novelty of which hadn't yet worn off, at least as far as I was concerned. "A conversation we should have in person," he reminded me, but his tone was light. It was going to be okay. I felt a rush of warmth that could probably be called happiness; I'd been a little too close to the precipice there for comfort.

He slid onto the stool next to mine in a single graceful movement and smiled pleasantly at Carole, who served him with alacrity. Straight women and gay men always do. I picked up my wine and we clinked glasses. "When did you get into town?"

"A couple of hours ago," he said. "Checked in with Ibsen, had a coffee with Mirela, waited for your wedding to be over. Mike wanted me to go look at the float, but I figured *la bella signorina* would want to show me herself." When he's feeling romantic, Ali lapses into Italian. Always has. I still have no idea why.

"Not much to see, yet." I was smiling like an idiot. I hadn't realized how really frightened I'd been. It was going to be all right after all. I couldn't quite get that out of my head.

"Well," he said, sipping his ginger ale and regarding me over the rim of his glass, "I'm here for two days."

"Immigration and Customs Enforcement can spare you that long?"

He made a face. "Personal days. Even government workers get them."

"I'm not complaining," I said, and drank some wine, then took a deep breath. "Ali, I'm sorry about—"

73

"Stop," he said, his fingertips on my lips. "It's fine. We're fine. It's tricky and we're probably going to argue some more before we're through it, but we'll get through it." He paused, then added, "But there's one really important question that needs to be settled now."

My stomach did a small flip. "What?"

He smiled for Carole. "Where we're having dinner tonight," he said.

***

In the end we picked up a pizza from Twisted on Commercial Street and took it home. The air conditioner was holding its own. Ibsen took one look at Ali and did his usual oh-my-gosh-I-like-him-better-then-I-like-you routine—Ali charms people and pets alike—and scrunched next to him on the sofa. I sat on the floor on the other side of the coffee table and opened the box. The Empire house special: sweet sausage, pepperoni, mozzarella, fresh mushrooms, black olives, peppers, and onions. Heaven on a pie.

"So," I said, through a mouthful of cheese, "tell me about Karen."

He drank some ginger ale. "I think things are getting a little rough for her," he said. "At work, I mean; I don't really know what's going on in her personal life. If anything. But I think the job's—not too much, not for Karen, but particularly demanding right now. She's been talking about it some, but..." He was looking decidedly uncomfortable.

"But what?"

He met my eyes. "This is highly confidential," he cautioned.

I nodded. I'm used to highly confidential. My boyfriend is an ICE agent. "Okay."

He didn't need me to swear to secrecy on a Bible or anything like that. "I'm not even sure how much I can talk about, but she's—she's been doing some work lately kind of outside her job description." He thought for a moment, while my imagination went wild. "Anyway... it's really not for me to talk about, she's dealing with it. She'll probably tell you about it. Maybe or maybe not. What I will tell you is— and it's not clear whether this is related to what she's been doing or not, but last week she received a death threat."

"Okay." I swallowed a bite of pizza. Somehow it wasn't what I'd expected. "Is that really unusual? I mean, no offense to Karen or anything, but doesn't stuff like that kind of come with law-enforcement territory?"

"It does," he conceded. "But this one's the sort we take seriously: it's very specific as to means and timeframe, and it's also very specific in being connected to her being Muslim. And a woman." He seemed to catch himself then, and I could have sworn he was going to say something else, but he changed gears. "So anyway, she's ready for a week away, and in fact she's up for spending a week someplace where no one would imagine she'd be."

"We can definitely give her that," I said, nodding. "Though she should know—well, it gets pretty crazy here." Not to mention *me* getting a little crazy, but that was my problem, and I was going to truly be on my best behavior. Maybe this was the year Karen and I would become close friends, who knew? We could hang out and talk about… there was the problem. Aside from Ali, we didn't have much in common. I couldn't imagine the demands of her job, and even though she'd never said it, I had the feeling she thought mine a little frivolous. Or maybe that was just projection. Maybe I'd find out next week, when she came for Carnival.

There was a thought: Carnival and heat. Poor Karen… if it was this hot here for *me* this summer, I couldn't imagine the scarf and the long dress or trousers, the long sleeves on the

76

blouse she'd be wearing... I felt hotter just thinking about it.

"I think she'll be fine," Ali was saying. "Everyone gets a little crazy for Carnival. She can lose herself and all her problems here." He helped himself to another slice of pizza. "She really just needs a change of scenery. A change of pace. People around her she's not responsible for."

"As long as she knows how hot it is," I said feelingly.

"She'll be fine." But he said it distractedly and wouldn't look at me, and the little claw of fear started dancing in my stomach again. "Ali? What is it?" I paused and he didn't say anything. "What is it you're not telling me?"

A quick glance, and then he made a decision. "And—well, okay, it's just I've gotten one of them, too."

I should have been more prepared for it. After all, he works in human trafficking, and I'm reasonably sure there are a lot of people out there who wish him ill. But death threats? Specific—how was it he'd put it?—*as to means and timeframe*? "Ali—"

"Look," he interrupted. "I'm not trying to scare you. Most of the time, this kind of thing amounts to nothing. And if it isn't nothing, Karen and me, we both have people investigating it, right now, even as we speak. It's nothing to be scared about."

"Is she going to have to have someone here guarding her?" I paused. "Are *you*?"

He shook his head. "Not unless we request it. No one's gonna know we're here."

"No one's gonna know you're here? The two of you don't exactly *not* stand out in a crowd, you know."

He looked at me skeptically. "During *Carnival*? You've got to be kidding. There will be middle-aged men dressed as Wonder Woman—"

"Yes, but—"

"There will be cowboys from strip shows. Little Bo-Peep. Lots of foreign-looking costumes. We'll be safe as houses."

"Yes, but—"

"Where else could I be safer?"

In a locked building, I thought. Surrounded by armed guards. I shook the thoughts from my head: that's a prison, Sydney, not a life. I tried another tack. "Tell me what they said."

"Sorry?"

"The death threats. The one against you, anyway. Tell me what it said."

"Sydney, babe, I don't think—"

"Tell me what it said!"

He sighed and pulled a napkin from the stack I'd brought from Twisted, patting his mouth before he continued. I suspected it was to give him a moment to compose himself. Or maybe to decide what he wanted to tell me. "They came through the mail, oddly enough, they're usually emails these day. Anyway, the mail, that makes it a federal crime right there. So the FBI's been called in." He could see that wasn't going to be enough for me and sighed. "What do you want me to say, Sydney? Give you the details? Really? Mine called for my head to be chopped off. Quote and unquote." He looked at me, suddenly angry. "Okay, so now you've got it. Did you really need to know?"

"Yes," I said, as steadily as I could. "I really did."

"Can we not talk about this anymore?"

He was still angry. Or upset. Or something. I couldn't get a handle on it. There was something going on, something under the surface, something not quite lining up right, and it felt like he was lying but I couldn't put my finger on the lie. "No, we can't not talk about it," I said. "We're a couple. There are things I need to know."

"And do what? How are things better now you know? The details made it better? How did that help?"

An errant thought blundered into my mind. "Are you trying to *protect* me? Is that what this is about?" Before he could answer, I said, quickly, "I'm a big girl, you know. I can handle it."

"I know." He dialed the anger down to a low simmer. "I just don't want you to have to. Handle it. Worry about it. Worry about me. We have people—"

"I know, I know," I interrupted. I couldn't help smiling. "Cold-eyed professionals with guns and cyphers and surveillance vans. And you know how much good that's going to do."

"It's what works," he said reasonably. "You know how many assassination attempts have been foiled, ones you never hear about? Four on President Obama. Two on George W. Bush. Four on Donald Trump."

"That's the Secret Service," I said. "Presidents get Secret Service agents. You don't have Secret Service agents."

"Nothing's going to happen, babe."

There was a moment of silence. "I can't believe you actually said *foiled*," I said at last.

A smile lit his face. "Why, aren't I usually literate enough?"

"Sounds like something out of a cartoon. *Curses, foiled again.*"

"Hmm." He wiped his hands and finished his ginger ale and looked at me expectantly.

"What?" I asked.

"Just wondering," he said, "if it's too early to go to bed."

I grinned. "Never," I said.

6

Ali came along to the inn the next morning. He knows just about everyone there, and he and Mike are pretty good friends, so I didn't have to worry about him getting bored. I was heading to the basement to look in on the float and talk to the volunteers I'd lined up for decoration. We had less than a week to go. I know some of the organizations, especially the nonprofits that never have enough time to breathe, much less create a float, put theirs together on the back of a pickup truck the weekend before, but that would make me crazy. I organize out.

The changes I was making weren't very difficult or time-consuming, in any case. Mirela had done some sketches for me as I outlined what I wanted, and in any case the foundation and the furniture (I'm sure there's float-terminology for furniture, but I have no idea what it might be) was already on. We only had a height consideration to be wary of, as pulling it out of the garage entrance to the cellar was going to be challenging, but most of the hard work was done. And people had been working off Mirela's designs for at least a few days now.

"Coffee first," I said to Ali, heading into the alcove where guests can use the Keurig at any time. Don't get me started on the Keurig, or the plastic it tosses into the ocean, which we find and collect when we do our semi-annual beach cleanups; Mike and Glenn were as one on that point. Convenience sometimes, they opined, takes precedence over ecology. Especially in the hospitality business. So I felt just a little hypocritical now as I selected a pod for coffee. I wasn't saving the earth today. "Do you want some?"

Ali grimaced. "After your attempts at Turkish coffee this morning? I have enough caffeine in me for three days."

"Attempts?"

"The water boiled over, you used super high-test beans, and you didn't serve it in the correct pot."

My turn to make a face. "I should know better than to serve Turkish coffee to a Lebanese."

"Lebanese-American," he corrected me. The flat-screen TV on the wall above us came on suddenly as he worked the remote control, and an overweight florid man on the verge of a heart attack appeared. I snorted. "Give me a break, that's not the way to start the day."

"I like watching the news," Ali said mildly.

"*Him?*" I said it with scorn. Cape Cod runs the gamut of political beliefs and political parties, from the Kennedy's Hyannisport and Provincetown liberalism to more conservative towns like Sandwich and Chatham; but we're all part of the same county, and Clark Thomas was currently running for sheriff of Barnstable County on a get-tough-on-crime platform. He was talking about militarizing police forces, cooperating with ICE, and generally enhancing his own political power. "He's an idiot," I said, conversationally.

"He's dangerous," said Ali.

I looked at him. "What do you mean?" My voice might have been a bit sharper than I'd intended; on the other hand, when someone calmly tells you their life has been threatened and then characterizes someone else as dangerous, it might be worth a listen.

"He knows how to talk to people," said Ali. "He knows what to say to scare them."

"Not on the Cape," I protested. "There's nothing to get scared of, here."

"Don't be fooled by what hasn't happened yet." He watched the screen for another few seconds while I tried to figure out what he was talking about, then he seemed to rouse himself. "I'm going to go say hello to Mike."

"Knock yourself out." I kissed him, then turned back to the Keurig. What *is* the right pot for serving Turkish coffee, anyway?

If I thought I was escaping the heat by heading down to the cellar, I was sadly mistaken. The team had mounted huge arc lights giving off heat like a Girl Scout campfire. I sought out Christine, who aside from being the inn's extremely competent head of housekeeping had also volunteered to be staff liaison for what everyone was now apparently calling Sydney's Float. "Hey, there. Nice progress. Where did we get the lights?"

"Tony brought them. He works for Michael at the theater."

"Who's Tony?"

She indicated a red t-shirt and jeans, which was about all we could see of the person madly applying paint to the sides of the float. Already this early in the day, the shirt was wet with sweat. "Aren't you guys hot enough down here without the lights?"

"They want to get the details right," she said. "To get the details right, they have actually *see* the details. Who knew? Anyway, I never noticed before, but they're right, it is pretty dark down here."

"Uh-huh." I sipped my coffee.

"So what do you think?" she asked. "It's your float, how's it coming?"

"It's not my float. It's the Race Point Inn's float," I said.

"Don't be silly. It's your float, Sydney," she said. "It's disingenuous to say anything else. The inn never did anything much for Carnival before you came. Now we have the float, and the special parade brunch—"

"Which Adrienne will never forgive me for suggesting," I added quickly.

She laughed. "Then there's the costume competition. The Inn never did much of that stuff before you came. And the costume competition is hugely successful, financially speaking, you know that. Mike loves it."

"He never told me that."

"He thinks success will go to your head."

"My hand's going to go to *his* head, one of these days," I said. "So show me around."

"Okay." We approached the float, which seemed very big indeed in the cellar but which, I knew, would look quite ordinary out of doors. It would still look like a float, mind you, and not just a decorated pickup truck; but it wasn't about to compete at Macy's or the Rose Bowl. Still, we'd won one of the awards the year before, so I did have a reputation to maintain.

It looked like this year wasn't letting me down. Instead of perpetuating the Disney Small World stereotypes, we decided to go back to the original idea of featuring places, and then just have as diverse a group of float-riders as possible, not dressed up in different outfits like kimonos or grass skirts or anything. Just people.

At the back of the float, functioning as a backdrop, was a nameless cityscape giving some height to the ensemble. It would be put in place once the float was out of the cellar; everyone made adjustments and changes while the floats were down at the Harbor Hotel parking lot, waiting for the parade to begin—and a long, hot wait it was, too, as one had to be there hours before lift-off, so to speak.

Along one side we had an Eiffel Tower, some pyramids, and Stonehenge; along the other was the Blue Mosque, a windmill, and the Acropolis. There was an elevated section in the middle—also to be put on later—with a buddha on it; and the riders would intersperse themselves as best they could around and in front of the world stage.

And what the team was turning out here was more beautiful than I'd ever imagined. The Blue Mosque was shimmering with inlaid plastic "mosaic" pieces; the windmill was actually turning—it looked like something Angus was going to want to make into a cake design someday. I went around thanking people and congratulating them on their fine work.

Michael Steers, general manager over at the Wellfleet Harbor Actors Theater, was in charge. "Hey, Michael," I said when I finally worked my way around to where he was standing, supervising the lifting of a Stonehenge plinth into place. "This is fabulous."

"Hey, darling." He kissed me on the cheek. "You like it?"

I nodded fervently. "It's amazing. It's just amazing. Even better than I imagined."

He was smiling, looking pleased. I like Michael. I was reminded of my first year in

Provincetown, when—despite having mixed feelings about the whole drag scene—I'd decided to check out a show at the Crown & Anchor. I was vaguely embarrassed by the whole thing, but was also determined to play along, so when one of the "ladies" came by my table, I tucked the traditional dollar bill into the top of her dress. She leaned down and breathed, "Thank you, Sydney." I sat up in shock and spent the rest of the night wondering how the hell "Anita Cocktail" had known my name.

Anita was, of course, Michael Steers. And a very nice drag queen he made, too.

I caught the same smile now. "You're proud of yourself," I said, accusing.

He nodded, unperturbed. "It's good work. Maybe next year the theater—"

"Stop right there," I said. "They're not poaching your float-creating from Race Point. They have you the rest of the year."

"We'll see." He turned back to the workers. "Dan, I don't think it should be at that angle. It might fall on someone..." and he was gone, absorbed back into his element.

Christine was at my side. "Better not let Mike hear that. He'll start hooting about insurance again," she said.

"It's a consideration," I admitted. "I'd better go have a word with him now. See you later."

I had something to tell Mike, and it was going to get him even more wild than worrying about a papier-mâché Stonehenge, that was for sure.

***

Ali was still in the office when I got there. Mike had conjured up orange juice and croissants from the kitchen, and they were laughing over something when I knocked and walked in. "Again," Mike said to me, "the idea is to knock, and then to *wait* to be invited in."

"We're still house-training her," said Ali.

"Very funny," I said. The window air-conditioner was whirring away. I plopped down in the other guest chair. "Did you tell him?" I asked Ali.

"Tell me what?" Mike sounded suspicious. As well he might, with both my track record and what we were about to tell him.

"It might not be relevant," Ali said. "It's not as if Karen and I were going to be part of the parade or anything like that."

"But Karen's staying at the inn," I said to him. "That makes it relevant."

"You two do realize I'm in the same room as you?" asked Mike. "I hate to complain in my own office, but I'm feeling left out of the conversation here."

Ali sighed and turned to him. "My sister Karen's staying here for Carnival," he said. "At the inn. We'll be coming down together on Saturday night."

"Okay," Mike said cautiously, drawing out the vowel sound. "And...?"

Ali looked unhappy. "Karen's in a public position," he said.

"She's Boston's police commissioner," I put in.

Ali shot me an irritated glance and went on. "And my job puts me in some—delicate positions, as well," he said. I wasn't about to touch that one. "The two might or might not be related, but we've both over the past month received an—explicit—threat."

"Threat? What kind of threat?" asked Mike. He was looking a little lost. The Race Point Inn isn't accustomed to hearing about anything more violent than a skinned knee on the patio or the occasional burn in the kitchen.

"The worst kind," I said.

He looked at Ali and back at me and picked up his smartphone. "Siri," he instructed the phone, "call Glenn, mobile."

"Calling Glenn, mobile," said a very sexy male English voice. I raised my eyebrows. Ali looked amused. "*What?*" said Mike. "Can't I have a little fun?" He was between boyfriends at the moment, his last one—who I'd genuinely liked—having flown the coop to Palm Beach.

Mike hit speakerphone. We waited through three rings, then Glenn's voice, gruff and impatient. "Yeah?"

"Can you come down here?" Mike asked.

"What's up?"

"You're really gonna want to be here," Mike said.

"Five minutes," said Glenn and disconnected.

I sighed and examined my fingernails. I didn't suggest we wait outside. I was sitting right in the path of the cold air and I wasn't giving up my seat anytime soon. Mike muttered something that could have been *Christ*, but it wasn't clear. Ali just went on looking faintly amused. He probably thought death threats were a normal part of life.

Glenn made it in two, which was good, since Mike's anxiety level was climbing. When he opened the door, the first person he saw was me. "No," he said. "No and no and no.

I'm not talking about getting central air right now."

Mike said, loudly, "It's not about the air conditioning."

Glenn came all the way in and caught sight of Ali, and his big face broke into a grin. "Didn't know you were here," he said and put out his arms. Ali stood up and they gave each other a hearty hug. Everyone seems to react to Ali that way. Come to think of it, everyone seems to react to Glenn that way, too. Glenn squeezed my shoulder with one of his bear paws; such was my rating in the Grand Scheme of Things. Just as well, since one squeeze came close to dislocating the shoulder. "So what's the problem?"

"You tell him," Mike said to Ali.

Ali sat back down and crossed one leg elegantly over the other, flicking some invisible lint off his jeans. "My sister Karen and I are coming down next week," he said.

"She's the police commissioner in Boston," I put in, again. All three men gave me a look. "Just trying to be helpful," I said, putting up my hands.

Ali resumed as if I hadn't spoken. "In the past few weeks, Karen and I have, separately, each received a threat of a specific nature. It's unclear whether or not they're related to each other." He paused. "It's also important to know we've both received them in the past, so this could be just coincidental. Neither gave us any cause to believe Provincetown is in any way involved. But we thought you should be aware of them."

"I see," said Glenn. He went over and sat on the fainting couch Mike keeps in front of the window, thus effectively blocking the flow of cold air from reaching me. I gave him one of my deadliest looks, but he either didn't see it or didn't care. My vote goes with the latter. He was looking at Mike. "You think it's gonna be a problem?"

Mike shrugged. "Above my pay grade to have an opinion about death threats," he said, then relented. "But if P'town wasn't mentioned..." His voice trailed off and he shrugged. He was playing with a pen on his desk and seemed more interested in it than in the conversation. He was sometimes that way around Glenn.

"We're planning on liaising with the police department," said Ali. "But if you're uncomfortable having Karen stay at the inn, under the circumstances, and you have every right to be, then we should talk about it."

I did everything but kick him. Wait, what? If Karen didn't stay here, where the hell did he think she was staying? On my *sofa*? I don't even have a bedroom door. Actually, I don't even have a *bedroom*, come to that; my bed and nightstand are in a recessed side of the main (okay: only) room in the apartment.

Glenn and Mike looked at each other and some telepathic communication passed between them. "I don't see it as a problem," said Glenn, and Mike added, "Just keep us in the loop if you learn anything new that might change things."

"Sounds good," said Ali. "We don't expect any trouble, but I wanted this to all be out in the open."

Everyone relaxed; you could feel the atmosphere in the room changing. "Damn," said Glenn. "Makes you wonder, doesn't it? You must be doing something right, to get people *that* pissed at you."

"I believe," said Ali carefully, "they think I'm doing something terribly wrong. But I take your point." He stood up. "Chances are nothing's going to happen," he said, extending a hand to Glenn. "But thanks for your support."

"Anything we can do, just let us know," Glenn said, shaking Ali's hand. Mike was looking at me rather pointedly. I sighed and stood up. "So you don't want to know about the float?"

"What's to know? Christine's keeping me in the loop. Which is better than the person in charge of the whole circus is doing."

"I delegate well," I said loftily.

"Don't delegate communication, or I might just forget about delegating paychecks sometime," said Mike darkly. I stuck my tongue out at him and turned to go; Ali and Glenn were already at the door, still talking together. "All right, enough male bonding," I said, slipping between the two of them. "We were about to go out for breakfast."

"We were?" asked Ali.

"Absolutely," I said and smiled sweetly at Glenn. "Want to join us?" He probably wouldn't; during the season he rarely if ever leaves the inn.

He surprised me. "Why not?"

I called Mirela and told her to meet us at the Post Office Café, one of the most central spots in town... which also has excellent breakfasts. I let her take care of giving them a call; she probably knew someone there who would get us VIP seating. Mirela knows someone everywhere.

She was only mildly surprised to see Glenn with us. "I see the bear is out of hibernation?" she asked.

He grinned at her. Glenn *is*, in fact, a "bear," one of a group of large, hairy gay men who like food, fun—and other large, hairy gay men. He inherited the inn from another bear, Barry, his longtime partner and my first boss at the Race Point Inn, when Barry was murdered and dumped into the inn's swimming-pool, something we didn't necessarily dwell on with guests. I'd helped identify Barry's killer, but the inn's corridors still echoed with his absence.

We ordered breakfast—the café cutely insists they are "boxes" rather than menu items, to go with its former incarnation as the post office—with Glenn ordering Box 64 deluxe (pancakes with fruit, and ham, hash, and bacon, with two eggs on the side), while the rest of us chose boxes in the 70s: eggs benedict, eggs Schlossberg, and eggs Sardou. Mirela and I ordered Bloody Marys; Glenn got coffee and a mimosa; Ali settled for his usual ginger ale.

It was the ginger ale that started the conversation. "Don't you get tired of it?" asked Glenn.

"Of what?"

"Not drinking." Glenn believes in getting straight to the point.

Ali shrugged. "I don't really think about it," he said. "It's just part of who I am. I've never tasted alcohol, so there's nothing really to miss."

Glenn drank half of his mimosa in one swallow. "Your parents taught you that?" he asked. Clearly this was going to be the Getting-to-Know-Ali-Better Breakfast.

Ali took a bite of egg, swallowed, and nodded. "My parents are a lot more observant," he said. "Once upon a time they weren't, back when they lived in Beirut—but that was Beirut in the 50s and 60s." He shrugged. "It's different there now." Another sip of ginger ale. "Back then, it was considered the Paris of the Middle East. Women in bikinis smoking hookahs by the pool, a lot of parties, celebrities galore—like Brigitte Bardot—it really was the place to be seen. Cafés where people argued about philosophy, nightclubs that catered to just about any taste, even a hotel that was apparently a hotbed of spies. Beirut had it all."

Ali has this secret crush on Brigitte Bardot. Our eyes met for the tiniest fraction of a second. But Glenn was fascinated. I could tell, because he had stopped eating, and it takes a lot to make a bear stop eating. "What happened?"

"What always happens," said Mirela, wearing her world-weary expression. "War happened." She has a right to her cynicism, of course; the Balkans haven't ever been exactly conflict-free. No place has, come to that, but some places more than others. I think the U.S. is the only country that hasn't been occupied by a foreign government.

Well, unless you're talking about the *real* native Americans, of course. The Wampanoag probably have a different point of view.

Ali was nodding in agreement with Mirela. "There was civil war in Lebanon," he said. "It's why my parents came to America—well, them and about a million other people. To escape the war. And after the war…" He lifted his shoulders in an elegant shrug. "After the war, the country changed."

"How?" Glenn was enthralled. I elbowed him. "Your pancakes are getting cold," I said.

He obediently took a bite, but his eyes were still on Ali.

"Lebanon used to be a French colony, very western, and the new pro-Arab factions didn't like it. Plus, the state of Israel had just been founded and displaced a hundred thousand Palestinians. Most of them went into

Lebanon. It was a mess." He shook his head. "Just because someone draws national borders doesn't mean people can be confined, or even *identified*, that easily."

"What side were your parents on?"

"Neither," said Ali. "They were Muslim, sure, but they were educated—my father was a law professor, my mother was an engineer. That meant they were philosophically pro-west, and when they saw how things were going, they left. But then, once immigrants come here..." His voice trailed off.

Mirela was nodding; she knew all about this. "We either become completely American, or we become even more deeply who we were before," she said. She'd chosen the former route; Ali's parents the latter.

Ali nodded too. "They'd been Muslim the same way a lot of people were. In Beirut, they went to shows and drank martinis and thought nothing of it." He shrugged lightly. "But when middle-easterners came here, they looked for other people like them. My mother started dressing differently, they started going to the mosque, the whole thing."

"So that's the way you were brought up." Glenn went back to his breakfast.

Ali finished chewing the bite of egg he'd taken as soon as he could catch a breath, and nodded again. "Well, it's why I've never had alcohol," he said, and smiled. "A long answer to a short question."

"And," I said, "his sister Karen was just as western as Ali, until she went to Beirut a couple of years ago and found the extended family there had regressed."

"It is not fair, to use that word," protested Mirela. "It is not a regression to go back to one's roots."

"It's a regression to go back to a time before women were permitted to divorce their husbands or own property," I said.

"It is about finding a balance, I think," said Ali without looking at me; we'd had this discussion before. "Between the culture of being an Arab and the good things learned from the west. It takes time to find that kind of balance."

"The war's been over a long time, Ali," I said.

"And cultures take even longer to settle, but in the Middle East? Thirty years is nothing. This is the cradle of civilization."

Glenn had finished his heaping plate and had started on his coffee. "So tell me about Karen," he said.

"She's brilliant," said her brother seriously. "She smart and thoughtful and cares deeply about her work. It wasn't easy for her to move up through the ranks; she's like me, we look foreign, and the cop shop's an old boys' network. She took a lot of grief., everything from being excluded from meetings to being everyone's second choice for partner. They gave her a really hard time, but she stayed strong and—and noble, if that makes any sense—through it all, and she never gave up. She took everything they could throw at her. They told her sexist jokes, sometimes really crude ones, and expected her to laugh. They'd give her a casual slap on the rear, and if she said anything, they'd say she didn't have a sense of humor. Sometimes they left tampons in her locker or desk drawer. And now she's commissioner."

"She's even stronger than other women would be in her place," I added. "When she came back from Lebanon, she'd started wearing a headscarf. Any grief she got as a woman, she got even more after that. She really is impressive."

"Because she wore the hijab? Doesn't she have to?"

"Not all Muslim women do," Ali said, and sighed. He wiped his mouth and put his napkin down onto the table very deliberately and very slowly. He cleared his throat. "Some wear a headscarf, some don't," he said at length. "Hijab means something else."

"What?"

"It means separation; a screen. It's only when the fundamentalist clerics really got going that it started being used for women's clothing. That wasn't what Mohammed meant."

He stopped as the waiter took brought another round of coffee. We weren't at prime breakfast time, so there was no rush; it was a good feeling, one you didn't feel often in the season, when turnover is essential for restaurants to make their money. Summer is never long enough, not for any of us.

Glenn stirred cream into his coffee. "So what did Mohammed mean?"

I liked this part. "Mohammed surrounded himself with feminists," I said. "His first wife was essentially a CEO. They met when he worked for her, when she was his boss."

Ali smiled at me. "And she's the one who proposed to him," he said.

"Probably had to do it three times," I responded, and saw his eyes light up.

Mirela stirred. "That is enough of a history lesson," she said.

"It's important to know. It makes a difference," Glenn protested.

"Only if you're a woman," I said.

7

"All this to say," I said to Glenn, later, when we were back at the inn, "Karen's made a choice, and it's up to the world to respect it, no matter what they think." You don't see much veiling of anyone or anything in Provincetown. We often go in the other direction.

Especially in the summer.

"I still don't understand why she wears—the headscarf," he said. "If it's not really required."

Ali had volunteered to face the crowds at the Stop & Shop so we could eat for the rest of the week; I'd avoided it long enough that the larder was pretty bare. Mirela had gone off to her shift at the gallery. Glenn and I had threaded our way through the extremely lively throng on Commercial Street. I thought I could see the heat shimmering off the pavement. Where you could actually see pavement through the aforementioned throng, that was.

Glenn and I were drinking iced tea in the lounge.

"I think a lot of women *want* to identify as Muslim," I said. "I think Karen sees it as kind of a badge. Like her uniform. It hits you right in the face when you see her—the uniform, the veil."

Glenn shook his head. "She's not wearing her uniform when she's here."

"She's not on duty," I said. "I think religion is more of a round-the-clock sort of thing."

"At least she won't be a target here, in P'town," said Glenn briskly, bringing the conversation back to its essentials.

"No," I agreed. The worst that could happen was probably that dressing modestly would melt her into a puddle. God knew I wasn't dressed particularly modestly in my short skirt and sleeveless blouse, and I was still hot as hell.

"We'll deal with it," Glenn decided. "I'm not turning away anyone from here because of

what they believe. Or because of any threat."
So he was still thinking about that.

"She's the Boston commissioner of freaking police," I said. "If she didn't get death
threats, she wouldn't be doing her job right." I
had no idea whether or not that was true, but it
sounded reasonable. Plus, being the Boston
commissioner of freaking police meant Karen
just might be able to handle said threats—and
any violence that might happen because of
them—slightly better than we would. I wasn't
really worried she was going to get killed in
P'town. My worries were much more mundane
than that. Like whether she was going to ever
speak to me again after a week in my company.

Glenn was watching the street outside the
inn. "Carnival," he said. "I wonder if it ever
gets old."

I followed his gaze. Less than a week to the
parade, and it could almost be already taking
place. Two guys walking arm-in-arm, wearing
American Indian headdresses and loincloths
(talk about stereotypical representation!). A
drag queen teetering on high heels. Someone
dressed like Alice in Wonderland. And inter-
spersed between them, the ordinary out-of-the-
ordinary sights summer brings: tourists slung
about with cameras and odd little hats, Bulgarian kids racing on their bikes from one job to

the next, a couple of men wearing far too little trying to cover up too much, a troupe of lesbians in sensible shoes, a girl with bright purple hair carrying an easel and canvas... People come here because they can be all the things they've always wanted to be. Outrageous, Artistic. The spark inside that languished for most of the year burst into flame in P'town. Everyone comes with baggage of one kind of another; but they leave, I like to think, with less of the emotional stuff than they had when they came.

And on that happy thought, I got back to work.

Ali stayed to dinner at the inn before heading back to Boston. He'd really only been in town to make sure things were okay between us. I don't know a whole lot of other men who would have done the same.

Adrienne our diva chef had outdone herself with oysters harvested that morning and cooked in a sort of Coquilles St.-Jacques dish in which they replaced the scallops, and I was sighing with contentment. Adrienne's probably the only person in my sphere Ali hasn't yet managed to charm. Her day will come, and I can only imagine what delicacies might result.

Ali was fiddling with his phone. "Work," he said, glancing up briefly from his texting. I sipped my wine, relaxed, and contemplated the chandelier so it wouldn't look like I was eavesdropping. I wondered who cleaned it, and how often. On *Downton Abbey* they were always taking the chandeliers apart, but the Race Point Inn doesn't have as many maids as Downton. I wondered how Glenn might like being compared to Lord Grantham. I wondered why the hell I was wondering about a PBS program that hadn't aired in years.

Ali was finished. "Sorry, babe," he said. "I have to leave now."

"Already?" We'd been looking forward to a slow stroll down Commercial Street, people-watching, and a drink at the Aqua Bar before he left.

"Duty calls."

I respected that; I had to respect it. It was one of our pacts. Work had to be allowed to interrupt; work had to come first. It didn't stop the stab of disappointment I felt. "Emergency?"

"Don't know yet." He was always vague with me about what he did. The specifics thereof. Sometimes I knew he was going to intercept a shipment, the occasional cargo container of people—women, mostly—from the Philippines or Eastern Europe or, increasingly, Central America. Sometimes I knew he was posing as a trafficker and going undercover. Sometimes I knew he was sitting in his cubicle in Boston doing paperwork. There was no doubt a whole lot of other stuff was going on in between I didn't know much about at all, and until he chose to share it with me, that was the way it was going to stay. "Could be. Could be a false alarm. But I gotta go."

"Of course." I stood up with him. "I'll go with you to my place—"

"No time," he said. "I'm coming back Saturday, I'll just leave my stuff there. You stay and finish your dinner." He pulled me close for a very fast, very intense kiss. "I'll call when I can."

"Be careful." I tried to keep my voice light. It had been easier to do before I'd learned he'd received a death threat.

"Three times and always." A brief smile and he was gone. All the women and most of the men in the restaurant watched him go.

I played with my salad and was thinking about calling it a day when Mike came in and sat down at the table. "I don't remember inviting you to join me," I said, mimicking his usual *I don't think I heard myself tell you to come in.*

"Don't want to let Adrienne's oysters go to waste." He was tucking into Ali's abandoned plate.

"Are you spying on us, or something?"

"A good manager stays on top of everything happening at the inn," he assured me. "Listen, how close are you to getting the float finished?"

"Pretty close," I said, taking a swallow of wine. "Why?"

"Last-minute request for a party this weekend," he said. "It's good people, people who've been clients for a long time. I'd like to say yes."

"What kind of party?" I asked suspiciously.

"One you can handle," he said. "One of a hundred that'll be happening all over town."

He was right about that. Except for the Independence Day celebration, Carnival is the most popular, most raucous, and most partying week of the year. It was about to open and there wasn't going to be a place anywhere in town where you wouldn't be within reach of some kind of party. Costume parties, drinking parties, dancing parties, sex parties, pool parties... you name it, it was going on. "We already have something going on here Saturday night," I said uncertainly.

"It's in the dining room, and you're not organizing it, so you're free," said Mike briskly. "We'll close the pool area so you have the tiki bar, the patio, and the pool. And maybe part of the spa."

I raised my eyebrows. "Must be very good clients," I said slowly.

"The best. Can you do it?"

"How many people? What do they want?"

"About fifty. And it's just the usual, Sydney: a bartender or two, music, light show, a photographer..."

"... and a doctor on call," I added, a little sourly. It sounded like the kind of party that involved more than just alcohol.

Mike shrugged. "Possibly," he conceded. I appreciated his honesty. "I'll deal with that."

"Okay. If you do, I'm in."

***

Saturday came and, with it, the official start to Carnival Week.

For me, Carnival always starts the same way. I never have enough sleep—due mostly to the fact of living above a nightclub, which makes for free house music at midnight—and I always start the day by getting on my bicycle and heading down to the Portuguese bakery on Commercial Street for coffee and a pastry. I try to avoid the Portuguese bakery most of the summer; I could easily gain about six hundred pounds in a season if I went there with the kind of frequency I dream about. The cream custard! The malassadas! The day it closes for the season should be considered a day of national—or at least statewide—mourning.

But Carnival... well, Carnival is special.

I took my coffee and pastry down to MacMillan Pier and sat on a bench and watched the boats while I breakfasted. The air was surprisingly sharp and almost cool, with a tang of salt and something underlying it, something edgy and giddy, almost like laughter. A nearby black-backed gull was perched on the edge of the pier, giving my pastry a sharp glance. "Forget it," I told him. "The tourists can come and feed you." At the price of these pastries, I wasn't letting a morsel go to waste. Or to gull.

It was a moment of reprieve, a moment away from Commercial Street—already working itself up to a hot fever-pitch that would last for days—a moment of quiet and peace. The first of the Dolphin Fleet's whale-watches wasn't going out for another couple of hours; the commercial fishing fleet was either already docked or already out steaming toward Georges Bank. A moment of quiet between then and now, between past and present, between the quiet of the morning and the explosion of energy in the afternoon. A moment I could claim as mine.

Let's face it: Carnival is ridiculously over the top. One of the things I like about living in Provincetown is I essentially live in two places: the winter, long and isolated and wild, filled with wind and twisted driftwood and the echo of lost promises; and the summer, exuberant and bursting with joy and abandon to the point of insanity. As soon as you've really had enough of one season—as soon as you can't face one more tourist or one more gray restless windy cold day—it's time for the other to begin.

And we were in full summer mode today; winter was just a smudge at the back of a painting, an abandoned memory, a leftover careless thought. The heat was intense, the beaches crowded, the streets a riotous clashing of noise and colors and excitement. There's an energy in P'town for Carnival week I've never felt anywhere else. Maybe New Orleans at Mardi Gras is like this, maybe Rio; I don't know. I've never been to those places. I just know the town was thrumming with anticipation, with the shared belief that anything could happen, that something marvelous could be just around the next corner, just around the next moment. It's a breathtaking feeling, the idea of standing at the edge of something unexpected and exciting, the sense that at any moment something wonderful could suddenly come your way. Some people get that feeling from drugs. I get it from my town.

High on Provincetown. I grinned suddenly. So much for subtilty, Riley. I drank the dregs of my coffee and stood up. Time to get out there and take it on. Come February, I'd treasure these moments.

There was a woman waiting for me in the lobby when I got to the inn. She stood up when I came in, small and graceful, the beads in her black hair bouncing, and it took me a second to place her; she was out of context. And then as though to remind me, my hand throbbed slightly, and I had it. The Outer Cape Health Services clinic. Dr. Madison.

"They said I could wait," she said. "I should have made an appointment to see you, but as it turned out I had a couple of cancellations, so I thought I'd take a chance and come by." She smiled uncertainly. "Thea Madison?"

"How could I forget?" I asked.

She nodded. "How's the hand?"

"Fine."

"You should come in to have someone check it to be sure."

"Okay, I will." We stood there awkwardly, the conversation—such as it was—dwindling in the air between us like smoke. I cleared my throat. "You wanted to see me?"

She seemed to come to life. "Oh, yes, well, I'm interested in your professional services, too. Can we talk somewhere?"

If she was expecting to be shown to my office, she was going to be disappointed, as I don't have one. "Let's go into the lounge," I suggested. "Would you like something? Coffee, tea?"

She shook her head. "Too hot," she said.

I led the way through the lobby and into the lounge, which was—fortunately—empty. "Have a seat, I'll be right back," I said, and slipped into one of the dining rooms where guests were lingering over the crumbs of Angus' pastries. "Stella," I said, catching one of the waitstaff. "Can you bring a couple of glasses of water with ice and lemon to the lounge?"

Thea was sitting in one of the overstuffed chairs when I got back, looking relaxed and completely at home. When she wasn't in her clinical outfit, she was wearing some sort of loose sleeveless fisherman's vest with cotton slacks and sandals, cool and unruffled. I felt large and sweaty next to her. "So how can I help?"

"Well," she said, "I don't know if you re-member, but I have this partner—Emma."

"I remember," I said, nodding. "You just moved to P'town together."

"Right." She nodded. "We haven't been together very long—just eight weeks." She smiled. "Almost."

She paused, as though waiting for some-thing, so I nodded encouragingly.

"Well, I told her I'd met someone who does weddings, and right away she said we should get married." The words came out in a rush. "She thought maybe meeting you was some kind of sign."

If she was waiting for me to say something like it's probably too soon for you to think about getting married, she wasn't going to get it. Fifty percent of all marriages end in divorce. It's not up to me to decide who's on which side of that fifty. I've seen some surprising matches that lasted forever and rock-solid ones that didn't. And then there was my parents. "Well, to start with, I don't actually *do* the weddings," I said. "I organize them, but I can certainly recommend an officiant for you, there are a few I really like and work with regularly."

There was a knock at the door and Stella came in with a pitcher of water and two glasses. "Bless you," I said as she put them down on the coffee table and left. I could feel the sweat trickling down my back; no one had yet turned on the room's air conditioner. I poured water and handed Thea a glass. "Secondly, I'm happy to help, but depending on how many guests you have and what you want, it can take time to get it all together."

She was looking amused. "I understand. It's nothing like that. We're too new together to have a lot of friends. But... well, what we were thinking, though... you have a float in the parade, right? I mean, your inn does. We were wondering if we could get married on that. Just the two of us, no guests. On the float, during the parade." She paused. "Emma's white," she added.

I was still getting used to the idea of someone doing anything serious on a float. "Excuse me?"

"She's white," said Thea. "And, well, that's not exactly Foreign Lands, is it, but it's diverse. I mean, it won't detract from whatever you have planned."

I drank some water and thought for a moment. It would be one hell of a great advertisement for the Race Point's wedding services for sure, with the tens of thousands of people who would see it, not to mention the coverage we'd get when I sent out the press release that it was happening, it was just the sort of thing news agencies loved... On the other hand... "Why?" I asked.

"Why what?"

"Why get married in such a public venue? It's going to be noisy and hot and you'll barely hear each other, much less the officiant. Why do you want to do it on the float?"

"It was Emma's idea," said Thea. "She's been chattering on and on about the parade, how important the parade is, our first Carnival parade together, how we have to go to the parade... just like a little kid." She smiled indulgently. "She said this would be perfect. She said if we're going to take the leap, we should do it as publicly as possible. And what's more public than a parade?"

"Well," I said, "you certainly got that right."

8

I had to give the matter some thought, and I had to think quickly, because the parade was on Thursday and it was Saturday and the Commonwealth of Massachusetts has a three-day waiting period between applying for a marriage license and picking it up in time for the ceremony. There's a way around it, of course: a couple can go to Orleans or Barnstable and get a waiver of the three-day requirement; but even bearing that option in mind, we didn't have much time.

And no matter what I decided, I'd have to first clear it with the powers-that-be—i.e., Mike and Glenn.

Was it a good idea? The promotional aspects of doing a wedding in the middle of the Carnival parade couldn't be ignored. And yet... couldn't that somehow cheapen the event?

But in the meantime I had other fish to fry; as soon as Thea left I realized the time. I had a plane to catch. Or, more accurately, to meet.

Summer flying is a breeze, no pun intended. (Okay, maybe a *small* pun intended.) Boston to Provincetown on Cape Air takes less than twenty minutes, with the added benefit of sightseeing; some people have spotted whales from the air, or a pod of dolphins, though I've never personally done neither. Then again, I don't fly in the summer, I'm pretty much occupied on *terra firma*. (I *have* had a few very exciting winter flights—remember that we're talking a single-engine Cessna here—during which every single word of the rosary came back to me and got pretty much worn out by the time we landed, but those are stories for another time.)

I was a little early and spent the time in the air-conditioned terminal—thank you, God— chatting with my friend Jane MacDonald, who works for Cape Air and was also waiting for the flight so she could go out on the tarmac and guide it in. Cape Air employees at Provincetown Airport do everything: check passengers in, carry luggage, troubleshoot problems, do outside work. We're a small airport. Flights land and taxi up to within a few feet of the terminal building, and passengers take it from there. Jane's also—well, not "also," she's primarily—an actor, and was appearing in some summer production up-Cape, so we talked about plays and characters and directors until her radio crackled to life. "Flight's on time," she announced and headed outside.

I watched with some nervousness as the plane taxied in and the passengers disembarked. I wasn't ready for this. Maybe by next week I would be. Or next year. Or next century.

The plane was full, but that still meant only nine passengers, seven of whom were white middle-aged men, unremarkable from each other. It was the other two I was waiting for.

Karen was dressed for the weather, or as close an approximation thereof she could manage and still have most of her body modestly covered. Cessnas aren't air-conditioned and she must have been pretty uncomfortable on the flight over. Her head covering was bright pink and her tunic and loose harem pants a paler shade of it; they looked like cotton. Ali was wearing jeans and a loose white cotton tunic-shirt and looked gorgeous.

They came into the terminal with the dazed look afflicting most travelers, no matter how short or long the journey, Karen saying something to him in a low voice and him looking around, presumably for me. As there were only three of us waiting for passengers, this wasn't much of a stretch. "Hey," I said, and he pulled me close for a small moment and kissed me, then a quick release and swinging me around slightly so we both faced his sister. "Hi, Karen," I said, not sure if I dared hug her. "Welcome to Provincetown."

Karen's as beautiful as her brother, with black hair—not that I could see it right now— and dark almond eyes; she's almost a walking stereotype herself, the dusky Arab princess, something out of Kipling maybe. She was getting some side glances already from the few people in the room—the TSA agents, passengers waiting in line for Jane to check them in so they could board the plane as it turned around back to Boston, the taxi driver lounging by the entrance, and I was annoyed so I stepped up and hugged her whether she wanted me to or not.

The rigidity of her body assured me it was most definitely in the "not" category, but she was gracious enough; Karen does good PR. She knows the right thing to say at the right time, a skill I've never managed to master. "How have you been, Sydney?"

"Hot," I said, then bit my tongue; whatever I was feeling, she must be feeling tenfold. I was wearing a little-nothing summer dress, sleeveless and short, with my hair up in a very high ponytail to keep it well off my neck and back. But the truth was, I really was hot. "And crazy busy," I added quickly. I turned to include Ali in the conversation. "Turns out I might have a wedding during the parade itself," I said. "Right on the float! Wouldn't that be something?"

"Who gets married on a float during a parade?" asked Ali.

"Someone who wants to make themselves a target," said Karen immediately. Of course; she would look at the security angle first.

"Actually, it's my doctor," I said. "She treated my hand when I cut it last week."

"Sydney isn't accustomed to chopping vegetables," Ali informed Karen, winking at me.

"Funny man," I said. "Come on, the car's outside." Which wasn't altogether surprising—it's hard to imagine where else the car might be—but I was doing my best.

Walking out of the terminal building was like walking into a wall of heat and humidity. I refrained deliberately from looking at Karen to see how she was taking it, and instead helped Ali with securing the luggage in the Little Green Car's trunk and settling Karen in the front seat next to me. The car had been in the sun long enough to be baked through; it was a toss-up, though, whether it would be worth it to put on the air conditioning. P'town's small enough that by the time you reach wherever it is you're going, the heat or air-conditioning in your vehicle will have just started working.

I did it anyway and we headed onto Race Point Road and toward town. Near Beech Forest the trees were doing their summer thing of arching over the road so you feel like you're in a tunnel of green; it's lovely, and feels like something out of Tolkien; you can just imagine hobbits in the vicinity. I glanced at Karen but she was staring out the window, her mind obviously elsewhere. "How was the flight?" I asked brightly, and it was Ali who responded. "Good," he said. "We kind of took off in tandem with this big Southwest jet, the two runways run parallel to each other. One minute we were both there on the ground, then it was way faster and going way higher than we were. It felt like we were in a toy plane next to it."

I couldn't think of anything to respond to that, so I said instead, "You have one of the nicest rooms at the inn, Karen. Glenn—that's the owner—always reserves one or two just in case there's a VIP, and you not only qualify, you get a suite to go along with it."

She looked away from whatever had been absorbing her attention out the window, something I was pretty sure had nothing to do with Provincetown. It's hard to change gears into vacation mode; it must be even harder to do with her job. "That's kind of you both," she said. "But I certainly don't need a suite, not all to myself." I didn't know whether or not it was a jab at Ali spending his nights at my place, so I didn't say anything. No need to put my foot in my mouth twice in a row.

"You would have needed a suite if they'd sent the bodyguards, after all," said Ali. He caught my eye in the rearview mirror. "The City of Boston wanted to send Karen with a couple of cops to make sure she was safe," he said.

"It wasn't going to happen," said Karen. She sounded irritated. "It's my *vacation.*"

"It might not have been a bad idea, under the circumstances," said Ali. He stressed the last two words, as though sending her a message.

"Or not," she said coldly. I wondered what they were talking about.

"Is that standard procedure?" I asked. "Or is it because of the death threats?" Too late, I wondered if I was supposed to know about the death threats. Oh, well.

"It's standard procedure for me to have a driver and a bodyguard when I'm on duty and in the city," she snapped. Sore spot, this, for sure. "Not when I'm on vacation. Not when I'm not tending to City of Boston affairs."

"But just because this was the least likely place to go doesn't mean it would have hurt to have someone else around. Someone you could trust. Under the circumstances," he repeated.

I felt like I was watching table tennis with a weird set of rules to which I wasn't privy. "The least likely place to go? I'd have thought that would be Bermuda, someplace exotic and foreign," I said, brightly, trying to be part of a conversation I only half understood. "Or maybe Iceland." The latter sounded better to me. I even liked the name: Iceland. I could almost feel the chill. If I were ever able to go on vacation in the summer—yeah, right, like that could happen—I'd go to Iceland.

"Provincetown is just fine," said Karen. I hoped she'd still be thinking the same thing by the end of the week.

The air conditioning had finally kicked in and was blowing gamely on our faces and toes. "I thought maybe we could have dinner at the restaurant tonight," I said to the car at large. "I made reservations, anyway, if that works for the two of you."

"You don't cook?" A sideways look from the almond eyes. Maybe she didn't know there wouldn't be a charge for dinner and was looking after my budget.

"Not much during the season," I said. "Not enough time." Well, that and having a kitchen the size of a postage stamp, with miniaturized appliances—not to mention free access to Adrienne's culinary creations. I'm supposed to go home and cook spaghetti after that?

Not that cooking *anything* in this heat appealed.

Ali said, from the back seat. "Karen, you're going to be amazed at the food at this restaurant," he said. "And the desserts—the desserts are fantastic." He paused, injecting lightness into his voice. "Sydney, since we don't drink, we treat desserts the way other people treat alcohol. It's something to be inhaled."

Karen finally laughed, and I could feel the mood in the car lift. I dropped them off at the Race Point—there's no stopping on Commercial Street in the summer, parking enforcement is enthusiastic—and Ali walked her in, leaving his own bag in the car. I drove up High Pole Hill to the parking place I rent from the Pilgrim Monument and Provincetown Museum; I can park for free with my town sticker in any of the town parking lots, but the chances of finding a place in any of them were less than nil. At least on top of the hill there was a breath of air and I paused before plunging back down, savoring it. They were going to build a funicular to take people up and down the hill, which was a pity, rather; it was going to become less isolated.

Which was the point, of course.

Back at the inn, Ali was sitting at the bar in the dining-room, Mike perched next to him. They were both drinking orange juice and laughing. "Hey, babe," Ali said easily, slipping an arm around my waist.

"What did you do with Karen?"

"She's up in her room, getting unpacked. I believe the term she used was freshening up."

I looked at Mike. "There's air conditioning up there, right?"

"Of course there is." He looked irritated. "It's one of our best suites."

"If I were her, I'd never come out of it," I said. "Lord, it's hot. Did Thea Madison come and talk to you?"

"Doctor? Wants to get married on the float during the parade?"

"Wait," said Ali, looking amused. "You were *serious*? A wedding on the float itself? While it's going down the street and people are screaming and the music is cranked? You crack me up, Sydney."

"It wasn't my idea," I told him and turned back to Mike. "But it would be a hell of a PR coup for the inn," I said.

"That thought *had* actually occurred to me," he said, a little wryly. "I *am* the manager here. I *do* consider promoting the place."

"You got under his skin," Ali told me.

"Not difficult to do," I said, nodding in agreement.

"Oh, for heaven's sake," said Mike. "Sydney, I have to talk to the attorney and to the insurance company, but if you're determined to do this—"

"I wouldn't call it determined, exactly," I said to Ali.

"More like, open to the idea," he agreed.

Mike ignored us. "Then as long as they're okay with it, I don't see any reason why you shouldn't. You said it's your doctor?"

131

"My new doctor," I said, nodding. It was the least I could do, really, make her my primary.

"And you know her? You know the person she's marrying?"

"Not yet," I said easily. "In the same way I generally don't know people coming here to get married. You know the drill, Mike. We make the plans by email and phone, we meet when they get here, it happens. I'll meet with Thea and Emma—that's the name of her fiancée—tomorrow or the next day. Like any other wedding."

"And you can find an officiant at the last minute?"

I laughed. "One thing I can guarantee is finding an officiant," I said. "No one *ever* gets married during the Carnival parade. They'll all be available."

"Well, let me confirm before you do," he said. "I don't want anyone falling off the float and suing us."

"There are other people on the float," I pointed out.

"And we're insured for them," Mike said primly. "Get me those names and the name of your officiant and I'll make sure everything's all in order."

"He actually said that," I said to Ali. "All in order."

He took a swallow of his orange juice. "He did say it," he agreed.

"You two," said Mike, "are impossible." He slid off his stool. "Gotta get to work."

"Good to see you, man," said Ali; they bumped fists. I rolled my eyes and took Mike's seat as he headed off. "How's Karen?" I asked.

"I don't know," he said. "Shall I consult my crystal ball?" He looked at me and relented. "She'll be fine, Sydney. Relax. She likes you. It's going to be a great week."

"We hope," I said, and then, as the words sank in, "Wait—she likes me?"

He nodded. "She's not the effusive type," he said.

"You can say that again." I considered it. "Well, cool, good to know." I thought for a moment. "I didn't want to say it in front of Mike, but I do have a concern about this wedding."

"Aha." He drank some more juice, then turned completely on his stool to face me. "There's a story here. Tell Aunt Agatha everything," he said encouragingly.

I made a face at him. "It's just, it feels like a whole publicity stunt for the inn, and I don't want to look…"

"Ostentatious?" he suggested.

"Something like that. Thea's black, and her partner's white, and I don't want it to look like I'm doing the wedding for the sake of diversity. It's not performance art." I sighed. "But it *is* good PR."

He gave me the crooked sideways bad-boy smile he reserves for moments I need cheering up. "Be careful what you ask for," he said.

"No shit, huh?" I sighed and put both elbows on the bar.

He was right, of course. It would look bad either way, no matter what I did. I—and, by extension, the inn—could be accused of discrimination if I refused to do the ceremony. I—and, by extension, the inn—could be accused of staging a stunt if I did the ceremony. But of the two, staging a stunt would definitely be the lesser of two evils.

I tried to shake myself mentally. This was ridiculous. It was only a parade; it was only a wedding. I'd created the float. I did weddings for a living.

How difficult could this be?

9

Karen looked a lot cooler than I felt.
She was in another cotton outfit,
her green headscarf shot through
with the same gold threads embroidered on her
tunic and trousers as well; she looked like she
was shimmering as she moved, an oasis of cool
in a desert of heat. There were a few people
sitting around the room, lingering over coffee,
maps out on the tables, planning their stay; and
she positively turned heads when she came in
and joined us at the bar.

Ali slid off his stool and held it for her to
climb onto. I signaled to Becky, cleaning

glasses down at the end of the bar. "What can I get you to drink?" I asked Karen.

The dark almond eyes were limpid. "I don't drink," she said.

"There's orange juice," I suggested brightly. "Or coffee?"

"I don't drink coffee—" she started to say, and Ali put a hand on her arm. "Karen," he said, and whatever passed between them put a stop to wherever she was going. "Orange juice," she agreed, and I made an another-round gesture at Becky, who nodded.

Ali moved another barstool close and sat in it, and we all tried to look at something else until Becky served us and moved away again. "I'm sorry," said Karen to me. "I forget, sometimes."

Forget what? But Ali was watching me, and I nodded. "No problem," I said cheerfully and picked up my glass. "Happy Carnival!"

"Happy Carnival!" they both echoed, a little to my surprise.

Karen took a sip before setting her glass down. "I understand," she said to me, "there's an interesting art museum in town. Would it be possible to arrange a visit?"

"The Provincetown Art Association and Museum," I said, nodding. "Of course we can go. I don't know what exhibit's up right now, but it's bound to be interesting. And I know my friend Mirela wants to meet you, and she's an artist—a rather well-known one, she's fantastic actually."

"Thank you." She took a drink of her juice. "The first thing I need, though, is to stop by the police station." I must have looked a little startled, because she added, quickly, "It's just a courtesy call."

Ali said, "When one cop visits another cop's territory, they stop in and just let the station know they're in town. Just in case."

"In case what?" I stared at him.

He shrugged, but it was Karen who responded. "In case anything," she said. "Sometimes we can be helpful to them. Sometimes they can be helpful to us. It's nothing to be worried about. It's just what I said—a courtesy. It won't take long, I'll be as quick as I can."

"Oh, okay. There's no rush, really. I was just—surprised." I had a thought. "I have a friend there. Julie Agassi," I said helpfully. "She's the head of detectives. I can introduce you, if you'd like."

Karen looked a little amused, and I thought how naïve I must sound. Karen was a commissioner, after all. Julie was probably supposed to curtsy to her or something. "Okay, never mind," I said.

Karen put out a hand and touched my forearm. "No, that's fine, it's kind of you to offer," she said. "I appreciate it. But I've already contacted the chief of police. I'll be fine."

"Sydney probably has work to get to," Ali said. "Why don't I go with you? I know where the police station is. We can take a walk over together, and you can see a little of the town, maybe stop in and meet Mirela if she's in the gallery."

"That would be grand," I said, before she could say anything. "I have to check on the float, and make a few calls." I slid off my stool. "Text me when you're done?"

"Sure thing." Quick kiss, a smile for Karen, and I was out of there. If I felt so uncomfortable after just a few minutes with her, how exactly was this week going to play out? I shuddered to think. It wasn't even Karen herself, it was wanting her to like me and being super-busy... *Note to yourself, Riley: don't invite anyone to P'town during Carnival week.*

I passed by the front desk, where the new guy—whose name I hadn't yet assimilated into my mental contacts list—called out. "Sydney! Mail for you!" I waved a hand airily over my shoulder on my way down to the cellar. "Thanks! Later!"

The float looked stupendous. Glorious. Perfect. No one was there working on it for me to compliment, so I just walked around it on my own, admiring the book. The Eiffel Tower looked elegant; the Blue Mosque shimmered even in the uncertain lighting, and the Buddha couldn't have looked more peaceful. If this one didn't win any awards, there was something profoundly wrong with the judges.

Upstairs, I grabbed the envelope he'd left me at the front desk and shimmied back behind it to get to my own little alcove and find my list. There were eight weddings scheduled for August, each at different stages of planning and execution, and there were calls to be made and notes to be taken. Not enough to feel overwhelmed... well, almost not. Best get to it.

And it wasn't until nearly three hours later I remembered the envelope in my pocket and thought to open it.

***

"I got one, too."

I'd called Ali, but not until my hands had stopped shaking. A little. This sort of thing might have fallen under the category of all in a day's work for an ICE agent or a police commissioner, but it was something of a shock for a wedding planner, so I can be forgiven for having been taken aback.

"What are you talking about?" His voice was unnaturally loud; there was a lot of noise in the background. They were obviously still on the tour of downtown Provincetown.

I didn't want to say it, not with the lobby open next to me and people around; it wasn't something I wanted to make too public. I tried the handle to Mike's office, back behind my alcove; it was unlocked, and he wasn't there. I scooted in and closed the door. Leaning into it. My legs were shaking. "Ali," I said again.

"Yeah, babe, I'm here. What is it?"

"Ali..." *Get a grip, Riley.* "Ali, I got one, too. A death threat." The paper was burning in my hands.

He didn't waste time misunderstanding me, or asking me to read it, or anything else. "Where are you?"

"Mike's office. At the inn. I—"

"Stay there," he interrupted. "Lock the door, and stay there, and don't call anyone else. I'm on my way."

"Ali—" But he'd already disconnected.

My legs weren't doing a great job of holding me up, so I just slid my back down the door until I was sitting on the floor. I was still, miraculously, holding the paper, though I had no idea where the envelope had gone. Holy shit. So this was what it felt like, being a player in someone else's narrative.

I didn't like it. Not even a little bit. Added a wave of nausea on to the weakness in my legs, just for a little variety.

Time passed. I didn't move. Then footsteps and knocking way too close to me for comfort; I think I jumped about a yard. "Sydney!"

"I'm here." I grabbed the doorknob and used it to pull myself up. Opened the door. Pretty much fell into Ali's arms. "Shh. It's okay. It's okay." He kissed my head, smoothed my hair. "It's all right, I'm here, it's okay."

Behind him, Karen said prosaically, "Where's the note?"

Ali said, quickly, "Let's get in here and shut the door. Mike won't mind." He led me over to Mike's desk and lowered me into one of the client chairs. I was still holding on to the note and felt rather than saw the look that passed between brother and sister. "I'll take it, shall I?" he asked gently, prying the paper from my hand.

It wasn't much; if I'd been a public figure or a cop or a politician it probably wouldn't have fazed me in the least, though the presentation was dramatic: exactly what you'd expect of a classic ransom note or death threat, the letters not-unexpectedly cut out from a magazine, glossy against the plain white paper they'd been glued to. To me, the message was no less dramatic: "Don't go to the parade. They're trying to kill you."

"Who's trying to kill her?" Karen asked. Ali shook his head; he still had one hand on my shoulder, reassuringly, and he squeezed it now. "Do you know, Sydney?" he asked. "Who the note's referring to?"

I shook my head. "How did it come?" Karen asked.

"I don't know," I admitted. "Front desk— it was at the front desk." She turned and left the room without another word. Ali pulled up the other client chair so it was touching mine, sat down, and took both my hands in his. "It's going to be okay, *cara*," he said.

"Easy for you to say," I managed. "I don't know if it's a threat or a warning. I don't know anyone who wants to kill me." I looked up at him, feeling lost and very small. "Who would want to kill me?"

"We're going to find out," he said. "Probably no one. Probably it's just to upset you. It's not really a threat, is it? Just a warning."

"About someone who might want to kill me? Or are they trying to get to you?"

He shrugged. "Possibly. But don't worry. We're here. We'll take care of you."

I sometimes smooth over what Ali and Karen do for a living. Saying "ICE agent" these days isn't likely to endear him with anyone, and for some people "police" carries the same connotation. Depending on who I'm talking to, I don't always reveal their professions right off the bat. In this moment, though? I couldn't have been more relieved.

I was liking law enforcement. A lot.

Karen came back, wearing plastic gloves—where had those come from?—and holding the envelope. "Mailed," she said to Ali. "Probably has dozens of fingerprints on it." She had a plastic bag with her and held out her hand. Her voice was gentler than I'd ever heard it. "Sydney? Can you give me the letter?"

It was on Mike's desk. I turned to take it and Ali stopped me, his hand grabbing mine. "Just in case," he said, and Karen reached over and took it and put it in the bag. "I'll take care of it," she said. "Sydney, we have to go report this to the police."

"When you're ready," Ali said, quickly.

And that pretty much took up the rest of the day. Who knew death threats could be so time-consuming?

10

Julie was relieved, I think, that Ali and Karen were in town. "You have your own bodyguard," she told me. "Honestly, we couldn't do very much for you."

"I know." I was feeling both wretched and relieved. And the truth was, I *did* feel safe with them there. But the question remained: who would want to kill me? The note was pretty generic: "they" wanted me dead. Who?

We had a subdued dinner at the inn, despite Adrienne's fantastic Portuguese fish stew, which would normally have had me scraping the bowl; it's hard to have a lot of appetite when you're running names through your mind, wondering if one of them might wish you harm. "It's probably no one you know," said Ali, and he was no doubt correct. Odd as it sounds, it wasn't the first time someone had wanted me dead. In fact, I've had closer encounters with murder than most people.

What happens, though, is that when bad things happen, you put them in a room in your brain and shut the door. When I'd first met Ali, there were bullets whizzing around us up at the Murchison estate; the reason Mike had once fished me out of the harbor was because someone else was coming at me with a knife and I'd jumped. For reasons beyond my understanding, if there's a dead body anywhere in Provincetown, I'm going to be involved somehow.

Maybe it was the warning that made this time different. The anticipation. Knowing what's going to happen ahead of time. Waiting for it to happen.

Or not going to happen. "We take it seriously," Karen told me, "but the truth is people who send messages like these, they almost never act on them. They're trying to scare you."

"It's working," I said.

After dinner the street was alive, filled with Carnival-goers, laughter and the start of seeing people in costume, and for the first time since I moved to Provincetown I had less than no interest in it.

Karen declared herself ready for an early night, a book and a bath. She kissed her brother on the cheek and then turned hesitantly to me. "Thank you," she said suddenly."

I was startled. "For what?"

She smiled. "For making this all so easy. Ali probably didn't tell you, but I'm—I've never been terribly comfortable around you. It's not your fault—it's me. You seem to have figured out how to make life work for you, and I—I guess I envy that, so I haven't been very friendly."

I shook my head. "Karen—"

"No, no," she said. "I just wanted you to know that I'm actually liking you very much. Have a good night." And then she kissed my cheek, too.

Ali and I went back to my tiny apartment, and I stumbled on my way up the stairs, I was so tired. The nightclub downstairs was just revving up for the evening, and I opted for a sleeping pill, something I almost never do, and fell asleep with Ali on one side and Ibsen on the other.

Any other night, that would have been sheer bliss.

Two days passed completely uneventfully, at least in the possible-death department. Two weddings happened. The float for the parade got its finishing touches. And Thea invited us to her house for a cocktail party.

It turned out Thea and Emma were temporarily renting the beautiful—and famous—Octagon House in the west end, a place I'd long admired without ever knowing (or even wondering) who lived there. Octagonal houses were rather the rage in the mid-nineteenth century, apparently, and the whaling master who built this Octagon House in 1850 believed its shape would deflect storms. I don't know how well the octagon worked out for him, weather-wise, but it was still standing nearly two centuries later, so perhaps there was something to it. It was later a hotel and—I think—a nursing home or an institution of some kind. I'd have to look it up in *Building Provincetown*. For now, in any case, it was Emma and Thea's home.

I'd finally stopped looking around myself every time I set foot on the sidewalk. *No one is going to shoot you, Riley. You're a wedding planner. No one puts out a contract for wedding planners. Breathe, Riley; just breathe.*

The house's windows and doors were all open, and there were people out on the lawn

148

(yes: in the West End, some houses actually have lawns, which isn't exactly par for the course for P'town), sitting in wrought-iron chairs or walking about, drinks in their hands, chatting. There was someone drifting around offering a platter of hors d'oeuvres.

"Sydney!" Thea pushed a couple of people aside in her rush to embrace me. It was hard to believe we'd met only the week before. "I'm so glad you came! And this is Ali!" She didn't hug him, but only just: this woman had enthusiasm. She turned to Karen, who shook her hand. "You're a friend of Sydney's?"

Karen glanced at me, and I could have sworn I detected warmth in her smile. "I am," she said. I felt a rush of affection. I was genuinely glad she was there.

Thea was enthusiastic. "I'm so happy to see you. Let's get you a drink! What do you want? We have everything. And let's find Emma! Oh, you're here, you're here, I'm so glad you came!"

I looked around, impressed. "I thought you said you didn't know anyone in Province-town," I said.

She laughed. "Throw a party and everyone comes. People here from work… and Emma's got some guys staying with us, they've been here a couple of weeks. They may have invited some people; I honestly don't know a lot of who's here. You know how it is."

I did. It doesn't take much to feel at home in Provincetown.

Thea grabbed my hand and pulled us farther into the house. A small portable bar was at the back of the living room, a waiter I vaguely recognized from one of the catering services standing at the ready. I didn't really know any of them; all our weddings are catered inhouse. "These are my friends! Get them something, will you? I have to go find Emma!"

The waiter gave me a glass of wine and Ali and Karen a glass of ginger ale each, and we smiled awkwardly at one another. "You're friends of Thea's?" he asked politely. Well, I couldn't blame him; what else was he supposed to say? Comment on the weather? "She fixed my hand," I said, holding it up by way of illustration.

He nodded. "She seems to be a very good doctor," he said solemnly.

"She is," I said. "My hand hardly hurts."

We smiled at each other and then Karen turned and drifted away, and we followed her.

Ali was looking amused. "You know," he said in a low voice, "for someone who makes her living doing the social thing, sometimes you're just as bad at this as the rest of us."

I made a face at him. "I didn't see you stepping into the fray," I said.

"I'm an ICE agent," he said. "I'm not supposed to have social skills."

"I wouldn't say that too loudly if I were you," I warned him. "I suspect that in the summertime about a third of the workforce here is undocumented."

He sipped his ginger ale. "Not my problem," he said. "Not my wheelhouse, not my department. And even if it were, I'm off-duty. Provincetown," and he turned back to me, the dark fathomless eyes twinkling, "is most definitely recreational only."

Karen was watching us and rolled her eyes. "Are you two finished?"

"For now," I agreed, drank some wine, and took a look around. The living room was big and the owners had had the sense to not make it either too Provincetown-condo or Provincetown-chichi (two very definite styles). It was comfortable in the way an old house gets comfortable, with imperfect wide floorboards and slightly sagging sofas, a sense of lives having been lived, daughters slamming doors in adolescent rage, laughter over card tables of whist, gentlemen's cigars and port.

"There you are!" Thea had appeared, magically, in front of us, with a woman in tow.

"This is Emma. Emma, this is Sydney, and this is Ali, and this is Karen."

Emma was taller than Thea, with long straight blonde hair. Her eyes were a startling green and matched her sleeveless dress. "Pleased to meet you," she said, smiling. "We really appreciate you coming. And marrying us, too, of course!"

Ali gave me a look, and I gave him a little shrug back. I'd not made the decision for so long that I'd made the decision. A lot of my life seems to work that way. I was really, really going to have to nail down an officiant for them.

"Well, there's a lot we need to talk about before Thursday," I said cautiously. "But I'm glad we can do it." I only hoped Mike and Glenn would share the feeling.

"How did the two of you meet?" asked Ali, tactfully changing the subject.

"Like everyone else does these days," said Emma. "Online."

Thea linked her arm through Emma's. "She's a real geek. Spends all her time on the computer," she said.

"Well, something good came of it, didn't it?" asked Emma, and kissed Thea's cheek. I could just imagine Karen's eyebrows doing overtime at all these displays of affection, and I forced myself not to look at her. "What do you do online?" I asked Emma politely. "For work, I mean?"

"Oh, this and that," she said. "I code some. Made an app a while ago."

"She used to have her own video channel," put in Thea. "Back before I knew her." She made it sound like the dark ages instead of a matter of months.

"Mostly I hang out," said Emma, laughing. "Email lists and social media and message boards. Most of my friends and family are virtual."

"That's not true!" protested Thea. "You invited more people here than I did! And you have family in Portland, remember, you told me you all went out together to get those sun tattoos!" She smiled at us. "All I can say is, it's a good thing this house has so many guest bedrooms. Emma's friends couldn't wait to take advantage of a house on the Cape!" She said it good-naturedly, but I caught a slight undercurrent between them. Ali said, easily, "That's what happens. You move somewhere beautiful, and suddenly everybody wants to be your best friend and come stay with you."

"It can be a good thing," I added. "Gets you outside when you have to take them around and play tour guide. It makes you appreciate where you live more."

"That's true!" Thea said, nodding. "And Emma needs it. Sometimes I have to make her come out and see what time of day it is. And she's being modest. She's done more than one app. She's built a whole lot of programs."

Emma said, "No one wants to talk about software." Her voice was sharp. There was a long pause, then Karen cleared her throat. "This is a beautiful house," she said.

"Isn't it? We were so lucky to be able to rent it. It just kind of fell into place, moving here, me getting the job, us finding this house. I tell Emma she's magic, all these wonderful things happened once we met. Eventually we'll buy something, but it could never be as gorgeous as this," said Thea.

"It must be hard to heat," said Karen. "I used to live in a place with high ceilings like this, too. Have you lived here long?" I exchanged glances with Ali. What was this, some house-hunting show on HGTV?

"Haven't been here long enough to know," said Thea cheerfully. "We'll find out this winter."

Karen nodded as though that confirmed something, and put her empty glass on the closest surface. "I'm sorry, I have to go," she said. "I'm meeting Mirela." She turned to Thea and Emma. "So nice to meet you both," she said, and added, to us, "See you later."

Ali was looking bemused. "See you later," he echoed.

"Is something wrong?" asked Thea.

He smiled for her, that heart-stopping smile. "Not at all," he said. "My sister makes friends faster than anyone I know. So you're getting married?"

"Emma!" A woman came up behind me and screamed in my ear and I nearly jumped out of my skin. "Emma! It's been ages, honey!"

Ali took one look at my face and said something to Thea about taking a walk and pulled me outside. Quickly. "It's all right," he said quietly. "Sydney? Do you hear me? It's okay. You're okay."

"I think," I said, "I'm getting PTSD without having had the T."

"It's normal," Ali assured me.

"No, it's not," I objected. "You and Karen seem to be doing just fine." And it was true; I'd have never thought anyone could take a death threat with aplomb. If anyone could, though, these two could. "And don't tell me it's because you're used to it."

"I'll tell you it's because it's part of our jobs," said Ali. "Not yours. You have the right to be upset, *cara*."

"Why do you do it?"

He blinked. "Do what? My job?"

"No. Call me *cara*, sometimes." I was having trouble breathing; better to fixate on something else. "You're not Italian. You've never even been to Italy."

He smiled. "Have you ever *heard* endearments in Arabic? They sound a little like Ibsen with a hairball. When I was a teenager, I looked up what was the most beautiful and romantic language around, so I could use it on potential girlfriends."

"And you found Italian."

"And I found Italian," he agreed, nodding. "Still works, apparently."

I made a face at him. "Shall we mingle?"

"After you." He gestured gallantly.

There were some people there I knew, and a lot I didn't, which was surprising; one way and another, I know just about everybody in town, at least by sight. Some of Emma's out-of-town visitors, no doubt. We did the social thing, stepping in and out of chattering groups of people. Ali still had a look on his face that indicated his brain was multi-tasking, as though he were doing sums in his head.

"Let's go home," I suggested finally. "You're not having fun."

"Is it that obvious?"

I shrugged and waited to say anything else until we were walking up Commercial Street. "Karen's not meeting Mirela, is she?" I'd had time to work that out, at least.

He paused as we navigated our way around a guy dressed as the Statue of Liberty, picture-perfect but with a dagger plunged into approximately where her heart would be. Subtle. Ali's gotten used to P'town; he hardly gave the statue a glance. "I don't think so," he said. "Mirela said she had gallery hours today." In the normal scheme of things, artists spend time staffing the galleries that show them. It's a nice perk for visitors, getting to meet the artist who created the piece being bought. "And I don't think Karen meant to go there." He shrugged, laced his fingers through mine. "Maybe something came up. Or maybe she just wanted some time alone."

"But she would have said so," I pointed out. I'd never heard Karen lie.

"I don't know," he said, but he had that faraway look again, and again I was seized with the certainty that something, somewhere, was wrong. That there was some sort of subtext I wasn't understanding, an undercurrent I wasn't grasping. Not just now, but since before Ali and Karen had even arrived. Something just under the surface, a spreading darkness, something moving forward, closer, slithering with a life of its own. There was a storm coming, I was sure of it, or perhaps something even worse, and it was closer all the time. And Ali knew it.

"What aren't you telling me?"

He slanted a look at me, and smiled. "That I'm starving," he said.

I shook my head. "Ali, don't."

He sighed and stopped, and we were an island, people flowing around us on both sides, shoals of fish not even bothering to see what the blockage was. "You have to trust me," he said. "I just can't tell you."

"Does it have to do with me? Or with Karen?"

"It has to do with work," he said firmly. "And I'm sorry I'm letting it bother me. It's Carnival; we should be having fun."

Yeah, that was my thought, too. "Whatever it is, you'll figure it out?"

"Of course I do," he said. "That's why they pay me the big bucks."

I wasn't getting anywhere, anyway. "I've seen your paycheck," I said, giving up. "More like, that's why they pay you the medium bucks."

"That, too."

11

We got the waiver to drop the three-day waiting period. Emma and Thea sat patiently in Orleans District Court while a judge sentenced a couple of DUIs and a possession rap, and then he gave them their waiver. There's never a question about granting it—it's a pretty archaic law, after all—and judges love doing it. "Are you kidding?" one court clerk said to me once. "It's the only time the people in front of them aren't criminals. They get to make someone's day. How cool is that?"

Waiver in hand, they came back to P'town and fought their way through the line of people waiting for the washroom at Town Hall so they could make to the office. Darlene, the town clerk, took the waiver and gave them their license on the spot.

In the meantime, I had managed, with Michael's help, to find a collapsible wedding bower we could raise for the ceremony itself, and had secured Dianne Kopser's services as officiant—it occurred to me to ask Vernon, a.k.a. Lady Di, but he was already presiding over the WOMR community radio float. Dianne, who was a chaplain at the Unitarian-Universalist meeting house, was less flashy but didn't get easily rattled, and I had a feeling it was a trait that would stand us all in good stead.

Ali was spending a lot of time on his telephone, and when I mentioned it, he just said, "work." This was, I thought, one hell of a vacation. He and Karen were both on edge, I knew I was reading that right, but I still couldn't figure out why, and they weren't telling me anything. "What's this problem they can't fix without you?" I asked Ali a little plaintively as we sat at the Aqua Bar and looked out at the boats moored in the harbor. "Do they do people-smuggling overtime especially while you're on vacation?"

"It's just a thing going on," he said, but didn't say what it was. I kept watching him. "Sydney," he said, and took a breath, and I knew, I just knew he was going to make up a story for me. He didn't want me to know, whatever it was, he didn't want me to know. "It's the usual, it's the port towns," he said, twisting his glass in his hands. "It's not just the location, it's the economy."

"Everyone knows there're drugs coming through," I said uneasily. "Not a lot, but some." Once, Provincetown's fishing fleet had covered the harbor; now it could barely cover one side of MacMillan Pier. "But you're worried about something more specific."

"I don't care about drugs," said Ali. "I mean, I care, of course I care, but..."

"Just not professionally," I suggested, and finally took a sip of my mojito. The Aqua Bar makes the best mojitos in town.

"Just not professionally," he agreed. "Look, let's not talk about my work."

"I won't if you won't." But it was like the place where a tooth had been pulled; you can't keep your tongue out of it. I couldn't help my feeling there was something here everybody in the room except me was getting. I looked out at the harbor, bright and beautiful, the sailboats at anchor bobbing like a child's toys in the bathtub; and underneath it all in the depths below I could feel that thing uncoiling, flexing its muscles, waiting for the right moment to break the surface.

Or maybe I've just seen *Jaws* too many times. Great white sharks have arrived at the Cape; they must be influencing my thinking.

I put my glass down. I either needed to stop drinking now, or drink one hell of a lot more. I opted for the former.

"Let's go home," I said. All at once, I wanted a shower.

***

By Wednesday everything was all set. Karen and I were getting along better than we'd ever done before, Ali was still being mysterious, and it had gotten even hotter. Ninety-six degrees with about the same humidity. I was going to be seriously surprised if I didn't just melt.

The float was gorgeous and everyone involved in creating it was completely exhausted. The plan was to move it after dark out to the parking lot of the Harbor Hotel in the far east end of town and leave it there overnight; it says something really good about all of us that no one thought we should guard it. There wouldn't be vandals; this was P'town.

No one had tried to kill any of the three of us; none of us had received new messages; it was pretty clear we could all relax. Well, besides whatever it was Ali and Karen weren't talking about. With all the noise of Carnival, it was easy for my fears to recede into the background. I didn't know why I'd been threatened, but apparently in such things—who knew?—motive is the least important element. "I could understand if it happened after the parade," I joked with Mike. "After all, once our float wins, there will be plenty of people who will want a piece of me!"

"That's not even funny," he said.

"Not even a little bit?"

"Gallows humor doesn't become you, Sydney," he said.

I idly picked up the copy of the Cape Cod Times from his desk. "Clark Thomas is making the front page now?"

He glanced over. "He's playing Nostradamus. Predicting what horrors are gonna happen to the Cape if he's not elected."

I flicked the page with a fingernail. "Murder and mayhem?" I asked lightly.

"He's being irresponsible as hell," said Mike.

"Why? What's he saying?"

"Why don't you read the damned article, Sydney?"

"Because you give better news analysis than CNN," I said. I was only half teasing him.

"Look, he's a nobody. Had a marginally distinguished career in the state police and retired when he got his twenty. He was deep into the political machine in Boston but never on the top tier."

"So what's he want with Barnstable?"

"Big fish in a small pond," said Mike. "Couldn't make enough of a name for himself in Boston, moved his family into the vacation house in Falmouth, suddenly he's all about making the Cape safe for the people he calls regular Americans."

"But there's nothing bad happening on the Cape," I said reasonably. "The opioid stuff, yeah, that's everywhere. But we don't exactly have hordes of barbarians stalking the streets at night."

"You just described his view of Carnival," said Mike. "Now push off, will you? Some of us have work to do here."

"Okay." I tossed the newspaper back on his desk and stood up. At the door, Mike stopped me. "Hey, Sydney?"

"Yeah?"

"Don't worry about it. It's Carnival. Don't fret so much. Take a week off from worrying and just enjoy it."

"Can I?" I asked softly, and left. But the truth was, it was easy to back off from the darkness because of the explosions of light on the street, in the bars and restaurants and the decks of boats, it was all around us. Say what you will about the tastefulness—or lack thereof—of the revelers, they were all happy. Giddy with sunshine and sea air and the kind of easy acceptance that's our stock in trade. Living the dream...

There used to be this trans woman who lived in town. She still had her baritone voice, and she used to walk up Commercial Street, starting way down in the East End, towing a child's wagon behind her, and wearing the shortest of short skirts, even when it was cold as hell out. The wagon had speakers on it, and she specialized in Sinatra. She'd set up in front of town hall and regale the crowds, many of whom wanted to be photographed with her... and this was in the days before selfies became a thing. Her name was Ellie, and man, she loved Carnival. She had a sign on her wagon: "Ellie... 72 years young... living the dream."

Ellie was gone now, her cancer taking her down the well-worn path of Provincetown's lost; back in the 80s and 90s, there were funerals every week as young and not-so-young men came here to die of the plague; but on days like these, with the streets awash in bliss and bursting at the seams with life, it was hard not to see their ghosts slipping silent through the crowds. Oddly enough, I never saw them when the streets were cold and empty in winter; they came back for the joy.

And this Carnival had more than enough joy to go around. "If it can enchant Karen, it can enchant anybody," I told Ali.

"You make her sound like a killjoy," he complained. "I've always told you she's a very nice person."

"A very nice person you've been super concerned about," I pointed out. "You were hysterical when she first came back from Beirut."

"I was not hysterical," he said. "You're right, I was concerned. But it all seems to have shaken out... She's doing well, she's happy, I don't have any complaints."

Neither did I. I was actually liking Karen a lot, too. "Buy me an ice cream," I suggested.

Darkness came, finally, and if anything Commercial Street became more congested than ever, people in costume walking up and down, hoping to see and be seen, the red plastic cups everyone knows contain beer ubiquitous as ever, laughter and music and every shop, restaurant, and inn blazing with light.

I didn't walk the float to the Harbor Hotel: Mike had roped me into a party at the Race Point and I had to make sure Adrienne's canapés were coming fresh from the kitchen to the outdoor area, to watch that no one actually fell into the pool, to generally play hall monitor for the fifty or so people carousing there.

Ali hung with me for as long as he could stand it and took off, Karen in tow, bound for some unspecified destination. Mike watched him leave gloomily. "I need a vacation," he said.

"You have Augustitis," I told him.

"Don't I ever," he said. "The float leave yet?"

"I assume so," I said. "It's dark out."

"But you don't know for sure?"

"Mike," I said patiently. "I'm throwing a party here, in case you didn't notice." Someone chose that moment to say something eliciting a roar of laughter from the group clustered around the tiki bar. I waited until the noise level abated. "I have minions," I told Mike. "I trust my minions. All shall be well, I promise."

Which just goes to show how really, really bad I am at predicting the future.

Ali and Karen got back before the party was even close to winding down, and holed up in her suite. I hadn't liked the look on her face, but I told myself it could have meant anything. There was something going on there, still, and it had gone from bothering me to actively creating a knot in my stomach. Their undercurrent was coming way too close to the surface.

I think about that a lot, those undercurrents in life. You can walk down a street and see certain things—something in a shop window you like, a person to wave to, general hustle and bustle—but you're also vaguely aware of something else going on, too, some kind of coded communication to which you don't have access, but someone else walking down the street at the same time sees as clearly as you see your friend or a shop window. It's an energy level, more than anything, and it's always fluctuating, because everybody on the street with you is bringing their own secrets, their own experiences, the things they're noticing, along with them too.

It makes for a crowded environment—all those thoughts, all those fears, all those ghosts.

I've walked down the street with Ali up in Boston and I was seeing Commonwealth

Avenue and the pizza joint we were heading for and the Green Line train rumbling on the trolley tracks beside us, only vaguely aware of people around us and how they were interacting.

Ali saw a drug deal. I never would have thought it was what was happening in that brief encounter, two guys giving each other the straight-man-half-hug, I'd thought nothing of it. Ali was experiencing something else altogether.

Well, okay, it's one thing to live in different layers of perception, and I don't actually feel bad I don't notice drug deals (turn me loose in a wedding reception, though, and I notice everything); but what was going on here was disturbing. Whatever Ali was keeping from me, I couldn't let go of it, a thread of anxiety weaving its way through my gut, telling me all really was not well.

Shut up, I told the anxiety. *Breathe through it*, I told myself.

Besides, I had other things to think about. I was really tempted to get on my bicycle and head over to the Harbor Hotel to see the float had arrived safely—there'd been no evidence to the contrary, but I worry—but my headlight was broken and I didn't like my chances in the east end with no light; the streetlights were few and far between out there. I toyed with the idea of walking up High Pole Hill and grabbing the Little Green Car and driving out, but that really was taking the mother hen thing a bit too far. Besides, I was exhausted; I probably couldn't climb High Pole Hill if I tried.

I wasn't even positive I could climb the stairs to my *apartment* if I tried.

And I still had to see Ali and Karen. Maybe they'd let me in on whatever was going on; I can dream. I made sure the people who were supposed to be clearing up after the party were doing so, and I headed up to Karen's suite. *Don't let there be a problem,* I prayed silently. *Just let it all be okay. I'm too tired, I've had way too long a day, tomorrow is Carnival parade, and... well, I'm too tired. I was too tired to think about being too tired. Breathe, Riley, just breathe.*

Which meant when the phone rang I was too tired to even register the caller ID. And it was, of course, my mother, up way past her bedtime, which had to mean crisis in some way or another.

I took the call.

12

I just thought you'd want to know the date," she said.

"I know the date," I said automatically.

"For your father's surgery."

Of course. The hip replacement. I probably should have called, except my father never speaks on the telephone. If he isn't out playing golf, he's reading the newspaper. Endlessly. My father has to be the best-informed person in the state of New Hampshire. Last Christmas I'd given him an iPad so he could read the paper online. As far as I knew, he hadn't yet turned it on. Maybe it's the rustling of the pages he likes. Or that keeps him awake, one or the other. "When is it?" I asked now.

"In two weeks." She took a deep breath. "Sydney, I know you'll say you can't come—"

"I can't come," I confirmed.

"—but it would mean so much to him."

If I knew my father, he would be embarrassed beyond words to have me anywhere near him when he was in bed and, worse, wearing a hospital johnnie. Truth be told, he was probably going to be embarrassed to have my *mother* there, too, but he didn't have any choice in that matter. For some mysterious reason of her own, it was my mother who wanted me there. And it didn't make a lot of sense. "Ma—"

She cut me off. "Your carnival will be over," she said, a note of triumph in her voice. "You see? I remembered. And that's what you've been so worried about."

Well, that and half a million other things. "Ma, it's not just Carnival, it's weddings. I just can't get away from work. Dad understands."

She made some sort of noise I interpreted as assent and changed tack. "I've been clearing the spare bedroom," she said.

They live in a five-bedroom house. But never mind. "Yes?" I had no idea where this was going.

"I probably should have put it in one of those storage places," she continued. "They're climate-controlled, you know."

It had to happen eventually: my mother was finally losing her mind. I looked at my watch: nearly midnight, the witching hour. "Ma—"

"It's my wedding gown," she said, getting hold of herself, her voice suddenly brisk. "I looked at my wedding gown again. Your father going into the hospital... well, I looked at my wedding gown."

I don't think I'd ever heard my mother sound as vulnerable as that. This time I genuinely didn't know what to say. I swallowed. "Ma, he's going to be all right. It's routine surgery, they probably do a dozen a day. He'll be fine."

"I know," she said in a tone that implied she didn't believe me.

I wondered what had gone through her mind when she looked at that gown, memories swirling in the lace and chiffon, the long summer days of their courtship, the nights sitting on the swing on her parents' back porch, holding hands, him with the beer her mother always set out for him, in his own special glass—my grandparents had heartily approved of my father. The wedding itself at the cathedral in Manchester, the confetti tossed all around them, and her laughter... I realized, suddenly, that my mother didn't do that much anymore. I couldn't remember the last time I'd heard her laugh.

And then she snapped back into the mother I knew and loved. Sort of. "Well, all I can say is, I just don't know what to do with this gown. You're making it clear I won't be passing it on to you anytime soon."

Good old Ma. "Not anytime soon," I said in cheerful agreement.

"It would be nice to be able to give your father some good news," she said. "If it's not working out with that fellow, there are plenty more fish in the sea. Carol Eastman's youngest just got a divorce."

Now *there* was incentive. "I have a boyfriend, Ma."

"He hasn't proposed to you, though, has he?"

"I haven't proposed to him, either."

"Well," she said, and I could hear the resignation in her voice, "you're not getting any younger, Sydney, and if you're going to persist in being with someone outside of the Church..."

I had a sudden absurd vision of Ali standing outside of a literal church and us waving to him from the doorway. Man, was I tired. "Ma, I need to talk about this another time," I said. "The parade's tomorrow, I just got finished with a big event, Kali's sister is here and I have to make nice with her before I can go to bed and get up early."

But it was late, and my mother's not usually awake this late. I eased up a bit. "Listen, I know you're scared about Dad. But I really, really think he's going to be fine. Why don't you go to bed? Take an Ambien if you have to. You'll feel better in the morning. Things will look different then." Advice she'd given me all through my terrible twenties, when everything seemed dramatic and immediate and important. Role reversal felt weird.

"I am tired," she admitted. At last, a subject on which we thought as one. Good. Time to wrap up my evening and go to bed, too.

But when I knocked on the door to Karen's suite, there was no answer. And I had to think that wasn't particularly good news.

***

I was awake well before it was light out; and these days, it got light around five o'clock. In the *morning*.

I won't say it was a premonition that woke me; more like a general feeling of stress. It was parade day, and I needed everything to go smoothly. I had a float. I had a wedding.

I had, it belatedly occurred to me, a possible death threat. Or at least a death warning. It might be a good idea to stay just a little vigilant here.

Ali was sleeping soundly beside me; none of this was going to make him lose any sleep. The man can sleep through anything. He'd been in the Navy, part of some élite diving crew, a fact he didn't let slip until we'd been seeing each other for at least a year. There, he explained, you went for long stretches without sleep, so your body learned to take it whenever and wherever. Three minutes of sleep, he assured me, could make all the difference.

"All the difference in what?" I'd asked; but he'd changed the subject and we'd never revisited it. It explained a lot, though, about how he managed to sleep through the merry-making in the nightclub downstairs.

I slipped out of bed, took a quick shower, put on my lightest sundress, and slathered myself with sunscreen. Carnival parade day was always an invitation to heatstroke. I had no hope today would be an exception.

Ibsen opened one eye; my running around the place clearly disturbed him. He snuggled back in closer to Ali. I was too busy to even feel insulted. Hair in a ponytail well off my neck. Tissues. Sunscreen. Sunglasses. I'd get some iced coffee somewhere; it was easier than coping with heating water and fumbling with the French press.

Ibsen had already closed his eye by the time I reached the door.

Downstairs I unlocked my bicycle—believe it or not, aside from the killers that seem unnaturally attracted to me, Provincetown's major criminal activity involves bicycle theft—and headed down to Commercial Street. On this busiest of all busy days, it was quiet, almost cool, shadows still keeping their secrets from the night before. Nothing was open yet, no tourists were milling about, no noise, and not even any heat rising up off the pavement as it would do later. Everyone was sleeping in, reserving their strength for the parties that would stretch on and on and on tonight.

Which was just fine with me.

I stopped at the inn; even at this hour, Angus the pastry chef would be pulling breakfast concoctions out of the oven, the kitchens filled with warm sticky yeasty air. I wasn't really interested in the pastries—okay, I lie, of course

179

I was interested in the pastries, but mostly I needed some caffeine in my system to get my energy level where it needed to be. The stress? It was taking care of itself nicely, thank you very much.

No one was at the front desk, and I slipped though into the kitchens where Angus ruled the morning and Adrienne, our diva chef, rules the rest of the day and night. There was a coffee urn right inside the door and I grabbed a go-cup and filled it. Black. Some days you just need to mainline the stuff.

Angus was in a good mood. "You're thinking you want something to eat?" Twenty years in America and his voice still reflected the sad cry of the curlew, echoing off the cliffs of his beloved wild cold Shetland Islands.

"Something like that," I admitted, and hugged his shoulders. Angus is always in motion; he doesn't go for long hugs.

"Cheese, almond, raspberry, chocolate croissants?" he offered. Warm from the oven, flaky on the outside, oozing with goodness inside. "You are a god," I informed him.

"Don't I know it, lass," he said, and turned back to his ovens.

I grabbed something filled with chocolate—in times of stress, a girl has to turn to something dependable—and headed out. The coffee went in the basket in front of my handlebars; the croissant stayed in my hand.

In general, riding your bicycle on Commercial Street is an enterprise that would put the most experienced slalom skiers to shame. Rik Ahlberg, who does all things bicycle in P'town, even teaches an actual class on navigating Commercial Street, and I wish more people would take it. But this morning, it was as though the heavens had opened and the gods smiled down on me. I passed no one but a portly man walking an equally portly dog.

I was liking this. I should remember to get up early more often.

The huge—by Provincetown standards, anyway—parking lot at the Harbor Hotel was filled with shrouded, hulking forms, all the people who, like us, had brought their floats over the night before. There was still a mist over the water—the hotel is directly on the bay—and a sort of sweet stickiness in the air, moisture with more than a hint of the heat to come.

There were pickup trucks with makeshift structures coming out of the bed; vans; even a couple of decorated RVs. We're pretty low-tech around here, and I seriously had to overcome a bit of smugness. So far, there was nothing to touch the Race Point Inn's entry.

We had this one nailed. I even pumped my fist in the air before I realized how silly that looked, a girl alone on her bicycle in a misty damp parking lot.

But we were going to nail this. We really were.

Our float was at the back of the lot, covered in tarps, impressively big and completely alone. The parade was at three o'clock; people began seriously lining up here around eleven or twelve. It was currently six-thirty.

So? I like to be on time.

I cycled over and started pulling at the tarps halfheartedly with one hand, even though I knew absolutely everyone involved would have told me not to. But this float was truly my baby. I'd helped design it, I'd secured financing for it, I'd had the original idea for it. I'll be honest: I've rarely felt prouder than I did in that moment, the takeaway coffee in my hand, the mist coming in over the asphalt and weaving in among the parked vehicles, the tarps covering Michael's gorgeous structures... A feeling of warmth and pride washed over me. I did this, I thought. I really did this. So much of the time, my job is so abstract: I make it through another day, another wedding, another event, another crisis... but this, this was enduring. We'd take pictures of it. It would win an award, by God it would. And it was *mine*.

I wanted to climb on it. I wanted to touch it. I wanted to feel it. And I just stood there, coffee in hand, still absurdly astride my bicycle, and just gazed. Nothing ever could take this moment away from me. In some ways, it didn't get any better than this.

By seven I was no longer alone. Mike had surprisingly arrived with a vat of coffee and a bag filled with Angus' creations and, even more presciently, a few folding chairs. We set them up in what was beginning to look like shade behind the building—the sun by then having made it through the mist, and the dampness drying out in the encroaching heat—and we munched companionably together. No one had yet parked anywhere near us, and we didn't bother to do anything to the float; just looking at it was enough. A few more people drifted over—Glenn, finally interested, and Tom Something, and the guy whose name I always forgot, but who had the correct license to drive the float. Thea texted me, "Today's the day!!!!" and Ali arrived with more coffee.

By the time the float exploded, we were all far enough away it was only ear-splittingly loud rather than lethal. I guess one has to be grateful for the small things in life. Like... well, *life*.

I don't usually spend a lot of time around objects that explode, so the experience was a new one. And in fact, there haven't been a lot of explosions in Provincetown itself, either, not since World War Two when the harbor was filled with navy vessels and the odd torpedo was taking out German U-boats right off the coast. So the float blowing up took everyone pretty much by surprise.

The fact that it was my float—well, the one I'd worked on, the one I'd had the initial idea for, the one representing my place of employment at the Race Point Inn—made its blowing up somehow even more personal.

As if someone trying to kill me wasn't personal enough.

P'town being P'town, a lot of the floats feature loud music and scantily clad well-oiled impossibly handsome young men dancing suggestively to a throbbing bass beat. Our float, I'd liked to think, was somewhat more subtle.

Apparently not subtle enough. Or maybe I just don't have a handle on subtlety anymore. I live in one of the least subtle places in the world, a town aggressively in your face about everything, a town with swagger to spare.

I'd like to add that, *technically* speaking, none of this was my fault. I didn't choose the summer's Carnival theme and I didn't really mean to interpret said theme in any way offensive to anyone.

All of which is easy to say after they blow it up almost under you.

13

It wasn't until later I learned about all those connections, of course. At first it was just pandemonium, or so I gathered: I wasn't hearing very well. My ears were filled with internal noise—nothing like the ringing sound described in books, but more like one continuous high-pitched hum, a buzzing, noisy and insistent, shutting out everything else. The blast hadn't been very strong; in fact, people said later it was clearly confined to our float and wasn't meant to harm many people at all.

I didn't know that then. All I knew was something had gone bang in front of me and I found myself lying face down on the asphalt of the parking lot behind the Harbor Hotel, gravel grinding into my cheek and my boyfriend pretty much on top of me.

The scene sorted itself slowly. It wasn't as impressive as it had felt; I heard later that people on the other side of the hotel thought it was a car backfiring. No windows were blown out. No one was hurt.

But someone had blown up my float. Or, more precisely, part of it. Later, I saw the jagged edges, the Eiffel Tower and Stonehenge in the bushes behind the float. It wasn't the most impressive bomb in the world, but I was quite impressed enough.

Ali was there and his hands were all over me, testing me for injuries. He kept talking, his mouth moving energetically, but I couldn't hear him. Mike and Glenn were talking, too, and I giggled at them. All I could think was how comical they looked, their mouths moving but no sound coming out.

"...all right?" I could finally hear Ali yelling. Somewhere in the distance there was a siren wailing; that got through, too. "What?"

"Are you all right? Nothing feels broken. Can you hear me?"

"I can hear you," I said, nodding. Once I started nodding, I found I couldn't stop. Bobblehead Sydney. "I'm all right."

He lifted me into one of the folding chairs he'd grabbed from somewhere. "Stay here a minute, babe. Are you okay if I leave you alone? I'll be right back."

I was still nodding like an idiot, and he took that for assent and took off. I saw him getting closer to the mess on my beloved float, his telephone out, already talking into it. Nice to have a boyfriend in law enforcement. I managed to stop my head from wobbling and wiped my hands on my sundress; they had pieces of gravel embedded in them. Another job for Thea, I thought, and then, oh, God, Thea, no wedding on a float for you today.

Julie Agassi pulled up minutes later, her lights and siren on. Glenn walked briskly over to her cruiser and began talking to her; she was listening to him but her eyes were all over the parking lot, seeing all those things only cops notice. A few other people had drifted over and were watching avidly. It didn't even smell like anything; I'd assumed there was something about bombs that smelled like gunpowder.

Not that I knew what gunpowder smelled like, come to think of it.

There was a horrible bitter taste in my mouth and I wondered whether it meant I was going to throw up. I'd tasted it before, and couldn't imagine the coffee or pastries had turned nasty on me like that. Later, much later, Thea would tell me what it was: the taste of adrenaline.

At the time I was just hoping I wouldn't get sick. And watching everyone moving around me as though there were a screen between us. They say you see things in slow motion, but it's not true: if anything, everyone seemed to me moving a lot and talking a lot.

Ali was talking to Julie. "I want to get her to the Outer Cape," he said. "She needs to see a doctor."

"Not until I talk to her," said Julie.

"I'm right here, you know," I said crossly. "I can hear you." And, wonderfully, it was true; I hadn't done my eardrums any lasting damage, anyway. There were a lot of voices now. Maybe I'd have been better off with the noise in my ears.

Julie turned to me. "What time did you get here?"

"I don't know. Six-thirty, maybe?"

"Who knew you'd be here?"

I shrugged. "I don't know, Julie. It was no secret. I told everyone I'd be checking it out first thing. What does it matter, anyway?" I frowned at her. "It was meant to go off during the parade, wasn't it?" Everything I know about terrorism—which is, fortunately, blessedly little, though not as little as I wish it were—is terrorists aim for maximum carnage. By that standard, this was a miserable failure. It was looking like my scraped palms were the worse injury here.

Certainly Julie didn't seem interested in talking to anyone else. "Did you approach the float at any time?"

"Kind of. A little, I was going to," I said. "But..."

"What? Why not? What does kind of mean? What made you change your mind? Did you see anything?"

"I didn't really change my mind. I hadn't made up my mind at all. It wasn't that thoughtful. And actually, yeah, now I think of it, I thought about pulling the tarp partway off to look. But that was all. I was just... oh, you know, it was a nice morning, I had my coffee, I was just kind of waking up and feeling dreamy about the whole thing."

"Dreamy?" She made it sound like a foreign language.

"Yeah. You know, Provincetown in the early morning, it's the best time to feel alive, and I was feeling it." She looked like I' just started reciting something from *Mein Kampf*. I tried again. "Well, okay, I was feeling *proud*. Proud of the float. Of all the work that went

191

into it. We were going to win a prize." And there they were, the tears pressing against my eyes. Damn it, we *were* going to have won a prize. Really.

"So you're saying nothing kept you from approaching it? From getting on top of it? Nothing felt wrong? You didn't smell anything, or see anything, that put you off?"

How did I explain this to her? "No. Nothing. I just didn't."

"It's a good thing," she said soberly. She turned to Ali. "Where's Karen?"

"On her way."

"Okay, you can take Sydney to get checked out."

I said, a little petulantly, "You don't have to talk about me in the third person, I can hear you just fine. And I'm fine, too. I don't want to be checked out. I want to know what happened to my float."

"You should be glad," said Julie, "you weren't on it when it happened. And I don't want you in the way, and I want to make sure you're okay. This isn't optional. Now—get."

I got. Sitting in the waiting room at Outer Cape Health, I turned to Ali. "I have to talk to Thea," I said. "I have to tell her. She can't have the wedding on the float now."

"Don't worry about it. You know Provincetown," he said. "She probably already knows."

He was right; between word of mouth at the Stop & Shop and the various community spaces on Facebook, the grapevine was alive and well here. "I have to talk to her about the wedding," I said stubbornly. "There's no reason it shouldn't still happen."

"During the parade?"

I shrugged. "Sometime today," I said. "Do you think they'll still have the parade? Will they cancel it, do you think? If there's still a parade, they'll have to bring in more security, this is going to put everyone on edge..."

He took a deep breath. "*Cara*, there are things you don't know about the parade," he said.

"Such as?" I'm suspicious when he starts any sentence with endearments in Italian. He's either feeling amorous or is about to tell me something I don't want to hear.

'There's excellent security," he said. "All the time."

"Yeah? Such as?" I asked again.

He sighed. "There's a SWAT team on call," he said. "There are helicopters available. And guys on rooftops."

Jeannette de Beauvoir

"Since when?" I couldn't remember ever having seen a SWAT team in P'town. We know all our police force by name, even the baby cops they import in the summer. No one wore their cap backwards or carried high-powered rifles. The closest I'd come to seeing law enforcement in black was Truro; their cops all look like they're ready to scale walls with a knife in their mouth at a moment's notice. Even the police *cars* in Truro are black.

"It's been that way for years," Ali said, and I couldn't help resenting him. I'd lived here a lot longer than he'd been spending time here; I should know more about the place than he did. Which was, of course, flying in the face of my usual argument, which is it doesn't matter how long someone's lived somewhere, everyone should be equal. It's the whole immigration dilemma in a nutshell.

I didn't ask how he knew. Law enforcement is indeed a blue fraternity. And he was also right—there were things I didn't want to know. A whole lot of things I didn't want to know, when it came down to it. Things that might keep me from sleeping very well at night. How many botched assassination attempts had he been talking about before? Not knowing things can be positively blissful.

I didn't say anything. The bad taste had left my mouth and I was feeling cold—a combination, no doubt, of shock along with the Outer Cape's heavy air conditioning. I was sure there was nothing wrong with me and we were wasting time. I also knew I wasn't going anywhere until I saw someone. That blue fraternity again; I wouldn't put it past Julie Agassi to hunt me down at the inn.

Given her line of questioning before, it wouldn't surprise me if she did anyway.

What had she asked me? Who knew I'd be at the Harbor Hotel that early? I'd been the only one around. Could it be coincidence, or was it connected to the note that was, no doubt, now being re-examined at police headquarters? I'd thought it was a mistake, poor planning, poor execution, the blast no doubt (and thankfully) going off prematurely. But what if it wasn't? What if it had in fact been times to go off when I was the only one around?

Or when nobody was there, which seemed a lot more plausible. I hadn't been on a schedule, after all. Maybe this was part of the warning, and instead of wishing me ill, someone was trying to protect me.

It was all too much for my brain.

***

The show must go on.

That's what everyone was telling themselves and each other. For most Carnival-goers, the blast was a blip, not even really registering on anyone's radar except as something to talk about, later, over cocktails. No one had been hurt; there was nothing to worry about. And Carnival was Carnival.

There were a lot of theories. I heard some of them when I got back to the inn, the most bizarre being it was the work of one of the parade competitors, wanting to put our float out of the running.

"You're kidding, right?" I said to Mike. I didn't have anything to do at the inn, but I didn't know where else to go. I didn't have anything to do anywhere. I had a call in to Thea. Ali and Karen had disappeared yet again. I had no idea where Mirela was. I fought an unhealthy bizarre sudden urge to call my mother. "That's just a tad extreme, wouldn't you say?"

He shrugged. "You know how people talk," he said. "By next week the story will be even bigger. By next year..."

"By next year everyone will have forgotten it," I said firmly. Or so I fervently hoped.

He ignored me. "No one was hurt, the parade will still be fabulous, it's summertime, it's party time, nine-tenths of the people in town today don't even live here. It's just one more thing."

"That's pretty brutal."

"It's pretty honest."

I drew in a deep breath and let it out slowly. This was turning into one killer Carnival, I thought. "Maybe no one was supposed to get hurt," I said.

He looked at me in exasperation. "Do you *think*, Sydney?"

"I don't know," I admitted. It came back to—why would someone want to kill me? Or was this about whatever it was Ali and Karen seemed to be dealing with in the margins of everything else?

I hung out in Mike's office. I didn't want to go home, didn't even want to be alone in the inn. Ali had told me to stay put, and I was nervous enough not to argue. I didn't care how much police presence was out there. I'm a wedding planner. We get sued; we don't get killed. This sort of thing isn't supposed to happen to me.

Mike was clearly irritated by my presence and just as clearly not going to say anything about it. It was an uneasy truce. Outside, as though nothing of import had happened, life went on. The day heated up. People were already staking out their places on Commercial Street for parade-watching—some with lawn chairs and umbrellas, others just standing about. By the time the parade started, they'd be three and four deep on what passes for sidewalks here. I stood at Mike's window and watched it all, safe behind glass, comfortable in the air-conditioning. And still confused as hell.

He gave up shuffling papers. My presence wasn't exactly thrilling him. "When's Ali coming back?" There was a note of faint hope in his voice.

"I have no idea," I said, a little blankly. I felt as though a brick had been pulled out at the base of a wall, and the whole thing was crumbling around me. When I got up this morning, I'd known exactly what my day was going to entail. "And Thea hasn't gotten back to me, either."

"She will," he said briskly. "They'll probably come over here after the parade. The day is young."

I was saved from answering by the desk phone. "Yeah, she's here," said Mike, not bothering to disguise his relief, and held it out to me. "For you."

It was Mirela. "Sydney! I have called and called on your phone, and left you voicemail. I am worried."

"I'm fine," I said. "Just some scratches." I didn't ask how she knew; it's a given that Mirela always knows everything. A thought occurred to me. "Actually, now that you mention it, I don't know where my phone is," I said.

"What are you doing?"

"Annoying Mike," I said. "Ali wants me to stay at the inn, and Mike's putting up with me."

"Babysitting you, more like," he muttered.

She gave something that sounded suspiciously like a snort. "I will be there," she announced, "in twenty minutes."

"Don't be silly, you can't even *move* anywhere out there," I said. "I'm fine here with Mike, really I am." Mike gave me an anguished look and I turned my back on him, leaning my bum against his desk. "It's really not such a big—"

I stopped. She'd already disconnected. I sighed, put the telephone back down. "That was Mirela."

"Yes," said Mike.

"She's worried about me," I said.

"Yes," said Mike.

"She worries about me a lot, actually," I said. "Sometimes it's like having another mother instead of a best friend. She used to say that—"

"Sydney," Mike interrupted. "You know I love you. You know I want the very best for you. But I can't pretend to care about the finer points of your relationships. I have work to do."

I stared at him blankly. "Work to do," I repeated.

He nodded encouragingly. "There you go. I knew you'd understand. So if you could wait for Mirela in the lounge—"

"Work to do," I said again. It was connecting to something in my head, the neurons fizzing around, trying to figure it out. Why were those words pushing buttons? It had to do with all this, somehow, and I couldn't quite manage the connection. Work to do...

And then I had it. When Ali and I had gotten pizza from Twisted. Standing in line, waiting, watching the television as the news reported a hate crime in Connecticut or New York or someplace I couldn't remember... and the idiot candidate for sheriff being interviewed about it, saying how our society was becoming too politically correct and how sometimes the violence out there was provoked and how he had plans to make sure no one was provoked into anything... and voices loud and entitled and obnoxious behind me. "One down," said one of them, and the other, "Forget it. We still have work to do..." They hadn't been skinheads, I remembered thinking when I turned to scowl at them; blond, preppy, two guys I'd assumed were gay, they were so neat and tidy. And then my number had been called and I went and got my pizza.

We still have work to do...

Mike was looking at me oddly. "Are you all right? Sydney? Are you okay? Do you hear me?"

I just had a terrible feeling that whatever the work was, it wasn't yet done. And they weren't in Charlottesville. They were in Provincetown.

14

Mirela came in like a tornado and bore me away with her, much, no doubt, to Mike's relief.

"Where are we going?"

"To watch the parade," she said, as though it were the most obvious thing imaginable.

"I can't. Ali told me to stay here."

She laughed. "We will stay here," she said. "Do I not think of everything?"

"I don't know. Do you not?"

We were heading for the inn's sweeping staircase when two state troopers in full uniform came in the front door. Of this day of all days, it would be easy to assume it was two guys in costume, and yet something about them, their stiff demeanor perhaps, made it clear they were the real thing.

They didn't even pause by the reception desk but headed straight for me. "Ms. Riley?" said one of them, cold and a little antagonistic.

"Can I help you?

The first speaker said, "We'll see about that. I'm Trooper Ben Gerace," and gestured behind him. "Trooper Mel Harvey." Harvey gave me a half-apologetic smile and nodded his head. He was probably used to mopping up after Gerace's verbal aggression.

"Okay," I said.

Mirela said, "I will wait for you upstairs. Suite 2A."

"Wait—what?" But she was gone. I turned back to the two uniforms. "So what is the problem?"

Gerace said, still aggressive, "You were injured this morning when the Race Point Inn's float exploded. We've been tasked with the investigation, and you're a person of interest."

"In the meantime," amended Harvey. "Someone else will take it on eventually."

"I'm fine," I said.

Harvey took a small notebook from his pocket. "We understand it was some distance away from you when the explosion occurred."

Gerace was looking at me as if I'd some-how magically made it happen myself. "As I told the Provincetown police," I said. "At some length."

"We have troopers going over the forensics now," said Gerace self-importantly. "We will determine exactly what happened."

"Go for it," I said flippantly. "Are we done here?"

"Do you have any enemies, Ms. Riley?" asked Harvey, almost gently. Almost.

"Of course not," I snapped. "I'm a wed-ding organizer." How many times had I said that in the past few hours? "I'm occasionally late with rent, but my landlord is pretty forgiv-ing."

Gerace didn't appreciate my humor. "Ms. Riley, you are not taking this very seriously," he said in rebuke. "It's enough to make someone wonder if you weren't somehow involved."

"Sure," I said. "I blew up my own float. I took one look at the competition and decided, hell, no, I don't need the embarrassment. Let's just finish it now."

"She just said she blew up her own float," Gerace said to Harvey. Harvey wasn't writing it down. He said instead, "She was being facti-tious." But he was watching me.

"It didn't sound that way to me," said Gerace. He was watching me, too. I remembered hearing somewhere that most cops don't have a sense of humor. Not on the job, anyway.

"You guys should take this show on the road," I said, trying to cover up the panic. I'm not used to uniformed officers coming to my place of work and implying I'd planted a bomb. Sometime, somewhere, this was going to get worse; I could feel it. "You're just too funny together."

"And you, Ms. Riley, are too unconcerned." Gerace studied me. "Tell me this. Why do you think it didn't kill you?"

I paused. It had been a pretty ineffectual attempt, and I'd already been thinking it wasn't meant for anyone, including me. A warning, perhaps; another warning. But even a warning was more than I felt I could handle. I considered a couple of flippant answers and then realized I was too scared to even try them out. "I don't know."

Harvey said, "Aren't you curious?"

I swallowed. "I haven't thought about it," I said. It sounded stupid. "Do you know?"

"Do I know what?"

"Why it didn't kill me." I couldn't play twenty questions; I was all out of answers.

"We're still investigating," said Gerace. "You'll hear in due course what the conclusions are."

Not if he had anything to do with it. I looked hopefully at Harvey. "Is there something I should know?"

He was impassive. "In due course," he said.

Gerace gestured to him, and he snapped his notebook shut. "We'll talk again," Harvey said, but he said it completely differently than Gerace would have done. Almost nicely.

"I'll look forward to it," I said. "Now I'm going to go watch the parade."

Before they could say anything else, I ran up the stairs to the second floor and to my surprise—though I have no idea why I'm ever surprised at Mirela anymore—Mirela opened the door to the front suite, the one directly downstairs from Karen's, which includes a modest balcony fronting Commercial Street. "You rented a *room*?"

"No, of course not," she said. "The guest is the owner of Tremont Textiles." I blinked, and she sighed and said in a rush of words, "You know this place, of course you do, everyone knows them, they do beautiful interior design work. In Boston. In the seaport. I am negotiating with him to provide some paintings for his showroom. And he could not be here this week."

Only Mirela could find someone with a view of the parade who was magically not available to enjoy it himself. I laughed, suddenly, and even though I could recognize the undercurrent of hysteria in it, it felt good. My mother might be falling apart, my float may have been blown up, and my life was very possibly in danger, but it was Carnival, and Mirela was right. Hiding in Mike's office wasn't accomplishing anything.

All the same, I scanned the windows across the street. Ordinary people crowding them, jostling each other for position. No one I could see on the rooftops. *And no black helicopters, either, Sydney, get a grip.*

Below us, the street was engorged with life, people, dogs, even some children. People in costume. People alone or in couples or in packs. A unicycle. Drag queens in finery that had to make them gasp for breath in this heat. Laughter, competing music, shouts. The craziness that preceded, accompanied, and followed the parade. Provincetown's own brand of insanity.

It's one of the few times during the year when I can look down the street and see no one I recognize. I leaned against the balcony rail. The sun was far too hot on my skin, but I didn't care. I was also probably presenting myself as a target Ali wouldn't like; but I didn't care about that, either. This, finally, felt more normal to me.

There was a knock on the door behind us and I turned, surprised. "I invited some people," Mirela said. "You should not be on your own, sunshine."

"I'm not on my own. I have you." But she wasn't listening; she was already at the door.

I don't remember how many people were there, but Mirela knows everyone in town, and she'd clearly invited half her acquaintants. I tuned them out after a bit. She was right; it felt better, safer, being here among people I knew. Michael Steers came over to commiserate together; Dianne Kopser, her wedding thwarted, was there; even Mike eventually put his head in. Mirela had organized Prosecco and, incredibly, leftovers from Adrienne's famous Carnival brunch.

The parade itself was, of course, spectacular. Insane. A little bawdy, a little rowdy, very much Provincetown. The ancient creaking firetruck duly brought up the rear and the spectators, released, surged into the street, yelling and laughing and that was when I realized, a little belatedly, that Ali wasn't there.

That I hadn't seen him since he'd dropped me off after the clinic.

I was about to tell Mirela when I caught a glimpse of Thea across the room. I couldn't not say anything, so I headed over. "I'm so sorry," I said to her. "We'll reschedule it."

She smiled. "I'm sure," she said, but there was something in her voice I didn't like. "What? What is it?"

She shook her head, and the beads in her hair rattled. "It's probably nothing. Pre-wedding jitters." She looked up at me and there was a glitter of tears on her cheeks. "Thea! What is it?" Then I realized what it was; no one can accuse me of being the brightest pixie in the forest. "Where's Emma?"

"It's fine," she said.

I grabbed her hand and pulled her into the suite's bedroom which was, blessedly, unoccupied. "Sit down. Tell me what's going on."

"It's probably nothing," she said. "But, well, after this morning—after what happened—"

"Go on."

"We had these wedding gowns," she said in a rush. "We just bought them. After we went to Orleans for the waiver, we went on to Boston and to Musette Bridal Shop—you know the place?"

No, but I nodded. "Go on," I said again.

"We thought, we're on the float, might as well do it right." If Musette was anything like most Newbury Street bridal shops, right would be a matter of about ten thousand for the two of them. Rock-bottom. Then again, I'm not a doctor or a software developer. "It was such fun. And then we came home and got the license and then got drunk on champagne." She drew in a long shaky breath. "We had them laid out this morning, ready to put on, when we heard the news. Oh, Sydney, I'm so glad you weren't hurt!"

"Thank you," I said. "Me, too. So what happened, Thea?"

"I don't know," she said. "I mean, that's the point, I don't know. Evvie—that's one of the nurses at Outer Cape—she called to say what had happened, because they didn't know if anyone had been injured and they wanted me on call if any emergencies came in."

"I'm sorry you had to hear it that way," I said, genuinely distressed.

She waved a hand in front of her, dismissive. "It doesn't matter. But it was clear—well, you know, that there wouldn't be a float in the parade today. And Emma—she just picked up her gown and put it in the closet. Never said a word."

I frowned. "I don't understand."

"Neither did I," she said, pulling a tissue from her pocket and wiping around her eyes. "I said, wait, we can still do it today. We'll do it here, we have plenty of space in the living room. It's not like we have to do it on the float."

"And what did she say?"

Another deep breath. Pause. "She said, we'll see. Just like that. Like someone speaking to a child. We'll see. What's that supposed to mean?"

"People deal with stuff like this in lots of different ways," I said gently. I didn't know either of them very well. "And then what happened?"

"She just went in her office and turned on her computer. Just like that. Like we didn't have anything else to talk about. Went back to her—whatever it is. Video games. Facebook. I don't know." She sniffed. "I know I'm probably blowing this all out of proportion," she said. "She's probably dealing with it in her way, like I'm dealing with it in mine. I'm just not sure I know her as well as I thought I did, that's all." She paused, then managed a smile. "Never mind. By tomorrow we'll be talking to you to reschedule."

"Of course you will," I said warmly. I was coming to like Thea a lot; damn Emma for doing this to her. "It will work out, you'll see."

She nodded and squeezed my hand and stood up. "I know. Thanks for listening. I'm going to head home. Maybe she'll want to talk, maybe she won't, but we'll work it out."

"I know you will." I followed her out of the bedroom. In the living-room, the party was still going strong. Mirela caught sight of me. "Sunshine, have some Prosecco."

I took the glass automatically. "Have you heard from Ali?" She nearly always knows what he's doing even before I do.

She frowned. "No, sunshine. Is he missing?"

My stomach gave a lurch. Missing sounded ominous. Missing brought back unwelcome thoughts of death threats and dangerous occupations. I pulled my phone from my pocket—Mirela had, of course, located it for me—and texted him. *Still waiting at inn. Where are you?*

Mirela was looking at her phone, too, "Nothing since one o'clock," she reported.

"This isn't good," I said. "Something's wrong."

"Perhaps, sunshine. Perhaps not. It is not the time to panic."

"Actually," I said, "I think panic is exactly what this situation calls for."

I pressed Ali's icon and listened as his telephone went directly to voicemail; either he had it turned off or had rejected the call the instant it rang. Not a good omen, either way. I scrolled through my contacts and pressed Karen's icon. Voicemail again.

Mirela was texting somebody. The little claw of fear was working overtime in my stomach. "Something's happened, I know it has," I said.

"Do not panic. It is Carnival," she said calmly. "People lose their telephones. People get separated."

"Not Ali and Karen," I said. "Not cops. They're careful. They're alert. They're trained. They don't lose phones. And especially not both of them."

"No," she agreed calmly. Mirela doesn't do panic, but there was something in her eyes I didn't like.

I took a deep breath to steady what nerves I had left. *Breathe, Riley, just breathe.* And then I called Julie Agassi.

And she answered.

***

It took us half an hour to get to the police station, and that was with me in a panic and not being particularly polite about shoving my way through the crowd. "They're here," she'd said on the phone.

"What do you mean, they're there?"

She sighed. "I shouldn't be talking to you," she said.

"Julie. What's going on?" *Breathe...*

"Maybe," she said, "you should come down here."

Now Mirela and I were sitting in the police station anteroom on hard plastic chairs. And Julie was taking her time. I was close to climbing the walls by the time the dispatcher buzzed us through to see her.

In the interview room—we were in an *interview room?*—Julie wasn't alone; there was a guy sitting at the table, deadpan expression, wearing a jacket even on this hottest of all the hot days. Cop was an easy enough guess; from the ramrod-stiff posture, state police. He wasn't in uniform, but he might as well have been.

He also looked vaguely familiar.

I ignored him. "What's going on?" I demanded.

"Sit down, Sydney," Julie said.

"Just tell me."

"Sit down!" I'd never heard her voice get that sharp. Usually Julie treats me with a mixture of affection and exasperation. I'm not used to her put-your-hands-behind-your-back voice, and I'd never herd it aimed at me before. I sat.

Mirela slid into the chair beside me. She didn't say anything, but reached over and took my hand, squeezing it.

I didn't need sympathy; I needed answers. I disengaged my hand from Mirela's grasp and leaned forward. "*Now* can you tell me what's going on, *detective*?" I asked.

"This," she said, gesturing to the guy on the other side of the desk, "is Detective Captain Thomas Norton. Massachusetts State Police." She paused, but he didn't say anything. "He's here to help sort this thing out."

"What thing?" Even to myself, my voice sounded unnaturally loud. And scared. I looked across the table. "What is it, officer?"

"Detective captain," he corrected me, un-ruffled. "We don't have officers in the state police."

"Fascinating," I said and looked away from him. Dismissively, I hoped. "Julie, talk to me."

He said, "You'll address your questions to me, and—"

216

"*Julie*," I said. "Talk to me! Is he all right? Did something happen to Ali?"

"Something will, if I have anything to say about it," said the statie. "Mr. Hakim is a person of interest in the investigation."

What? "What does that mean? What investigation?" My voice went up a few notes. "Julie! Is this about the float? What's going on?"

She stirred uncomfortably. "Just stay calm," she said. She might be my friend, but she was a cop first; I had to remember that.

I turned to Mirela. "Call a lawyer," I said, thanking heaven she was with me. If I'd been alone, I'd have had to Google local lawyers. Mirela would know the right one, and probably had them on speed-dial.

She nodded, stood up, and hesitated, waiting perhaps to see if she was going to be detained. No one said anything. She nodded, as if confirming something unspoken, and left.

"I have some questions for you, Ms. Riley," the state cop said. He reached out his hand to the side without taking his eyes off my face, and Julie put a folder in it. Not a muscle twitched, but I could imagine how much she liked being treated like an office assistant, and by a man, by a trooper, to boot. She was good, though. Her training kicked in even when her emotions were stirred.

I pulled my attention back to him. Norton? Morton? Why couldn't I remember names? And where had I seen his face before? He had the folder open in front of him, tipped slightly on the edge of the table so I couldn't do upside-down reading. It was a wasted effort; I suck at upside-down reading. Just ask Mike, all the times I've been in his office and wanted to read whatever he was lecturing me about. Not a skill I'd ever mastered.

He cleared his throat. "Mr. Hakim is a friend of yours." It wasn't a question, so I didn't say anything, and he looked up. "Is he?"

"I need to know where he is," I said. "I need to know what's going on." A thought hit—albeit belatedly, and I turned to Julie again. "What about Karen? Is she here, too?" I couldn't imagine it. I looked back at the statie. "Before you get in too deep here, you should know who his sister is."

"I know who Commissioner Hakim is," he said, clearing his throat again, a rumble that lent more weight to the words.

"And you're still holding her? This has to be a joke."

"Commissioner Hakim has been provided every facility," he said. "Commissioner Hakim is here as a professional courtesy to us. She is not currently being held."

"But Ali is."

"Mr. Hakim—"

"That's *Agent* Hakim to you," I snapped.

Julie said, "Sydney, you should know—"

He cut across her, fast and smooth. "Anything Ms. Riley needs to know, I will tell her," he said.

"Then tell me," I said. My fear was making me, if anything, more sarcastic and less careful. "You're not as scary as you think you are. It's not as if the state police have been so competent or honest or even legal these last few years. I'm not impressed." This was true; they'd even closed down the barracks that used to deal exclusively with the Mass Pike, because of all sorts of things going on, though I couldn't remember at the moment just what those things were. Cheating on overtime? Something like that? And hadn't some of the higher-ups gotten in trouble over some sex scandal? I thought I'd read something along those lines, too. It didn't matter.

He was professional; if he was remembering the same things, his face gave nothing away.

I plunged on regardless. "And now Mirela's getting him an attorney. So this is public record, isn't it? You'll have to tell everyone eventually. So tell me now! If you weren't going to tell me anything, why'd you drag me down here?"

Julie stirred and he darted another scathing look her way. She'd done it, called me in, despite him. I had to give her some credit for that. But it wasn't something he was about to admit.

He cleared his throat again. It was an incredibly annoying mannerism, and I didn't have time for it. For any of it. For his stupid games. For all of this to not be a nightmare. You'd think an explosion would be enough excitement for one day, but apparently not in Sydney's world. "Mr.—excuse me, Agent— Hakim," he said finally, "is helping us determine who planted the explosive device that detonated in the Race Point Inn's parade float this morning."

I stared at him. "You're *kidding*. It was my float. If anyone one was supposed to get hurt, it was probably me."

"And yet... you weren't."

This was Kafkaesque. "He's my boyfriend, for God's sake," I said. "And he's a cop, too. He wouldn't do anything to hurt me, hell, he wouldn't do anything to hurt anybody..." And then I caught his expression. "Oh," I said. "I

see. I get it. Of course. He's my *Muslim* boyfriend, so of course he's a terrorist." And then
suddenly I had it: where I'd seen this guy
Morton. Norton. Whatever. One of the
impassive faces surrounding the idiot Clark
Thomas on television when he'd done the
press conference to announce his candidacy
for sheriff. He'd been playing up his past as a
cop with a bunch of people around him in
state police uniforms. This guy had been
standing next to him. "This is right up your
alley, isn't it?" I demanded. "Convict the
Muslim for a bombing and get points for your
boy Thomas." I was having troubles breathing
again by the end of my little speech. What had
they done to Ali? What were they going to do
to me?

He went on looking impassive. I stood up,
nearly knocking my chair over in the process.
"I want to see him," I said.

"He's still being processed," Julie said.
"You can see him in a while."

"Why?" I meant to yell at her, but it came
out as a whimper. There were tears stinging my
eyes. Fear and frustration. "Why Ali? Julie, this
is absurd. You know him. You know he
never..."

"There was evidence," she said, not looking at the statie, who immediately added,

"which is confidential at this point. It is part of an ongoing investigation."

"I'll wait somewhere else," I said.

"Sit down, Ms. Riley." None of my little tantrums seemed to have any effect on him. Maybe they teach you how to ignore people at the state police academy.

"I want—"

"Did you spend the day yesterday with Mr. Hakim?" So we were dropping the courtesy title already.

I sat down and looked a little wildly at Julie. I should have known she was already pushing it a little with her colleague. "I don't—"

"What about last night? We're most interested in his movements between—" he consulted his folder "—ten o'clock and midnight."

"He was with me," I snapped. And then remembered. The party at the inn, running late. My mother's bizarre phone call. Ali and Karen being out when I went up to Karen's suite. Going home, bone-tired, and falling asleep accidentally on the couch. Waking up, cramped and hot, and stumbling into the alcove that in my apartment passes for a bedroom, Ali already there, sound asleep. I had no idea what time it had been; I'd stripped and crawled naked under the summer-weight duvet.

It didn't matter. Just because I hadn't known where Ali was, that didn't make him a terrorist. It was a coincidence. He and Karen had been out taking a walk, having a discussion, getting a late coffee, doing whatever they do, talking about whatever they talk about. God knew the streets were still pretty much thronged at midnight.

Julie was watching me. I didn't like the feeling she was reading my mind. "He didn't do this," I said to her.

"And yet a man matching his description was seen on the closed-circuit television recording at the hotel," said the trooper-detective. "Hard to explain."

"It depends on what you mean by matching his description," I said. "Arab? Is that it? Anyone who looks Middle-Eastern—"

"Sydney," Julie said, a warning in her voice.

The door opened and Mirela came in. "She is on her way," she reported. Everyone looked at her. "The attorney," she said. "She is on her way."

"Thank God," I said, and stood up again. "Any more questions, you can talk to Ali's attorney," I said.

Mirela looked at my face. "Come on," she said, pulling me out the door. No one inside said anything.

"They think Ali blew up the float," I said to her. The reality of it was beginning to sink in.

"I know," she said. "Do not talk here, sunshine."

"You think they're listening?"

She gave me a look equal parts incredulous and amused. "Of course, sunshine, why would the police listen to what you say in a police station?"

I was going to say something about it being America, too, and then I shut up. This wasn't my America, not anymore. If this could happen here, it could happen anywhere.

The heat and humidity made it feel like we were walking into a wall when we went outside; I'd grown accustomed to the dry chill of the central air. "Who is it?" I asked.

"Who is what?" She was fiddling with her smartphone.

"His attorney. You said she's on her way."

"Her name is Margo Nash. She is very good, sunshine. But... it will take a long time," she said soberly. "Her office is in Marstons Mills."

Up-Cape, then. Way up-Cape. Marstons Mills is one of those quintessentially quaint Cape Cod towns like Sandwich or Mashpee, towns that just look like everyone's image of

Cape Cod, neat and pretty, the kind of place you half-remember your parents taking you on vacation back before the Cape was overrun with millionaires building second homes the size of small countries. How Mirela had a connection there was beyond my imagination.

The bad news, of course, was it was up-Cape, an hour's drive away in February. In August? On a hot summer Thursday? With Carnival going on in P'town? We'd be lucky if she could make it in twice that time.

"Okay," Mirela said. "What do we do in the meantime?"

I'd had some time to think, and I wasn't liking my thoughts. "We need to talk to Karen," I said.

"Why?"

"Because," I said, "it's time she came clean about why she's really in Provincetown."

15

I pulled out my phone and pressed Karen's icon. The call went again to voicemail; she had to still be helping the police with their inquiries. Whatever the hell that meant; I winced at the officialese that even I was using. Short of camping out in front of the police station, I was at a loss as to what to do.

"Get a drink," said Mirela. "We should get a drink."

I wasn't so sure; the Prosecco we'd gulped at the inn hadn't weathered—well, the *weather*—as well as I usually manage with alcohol; but I didn't exactly have a Plan B. I was still a little dazed that Plan A had fallen through. This day had veered so sharply off course it felt anything could happen. "Is the parade over?" I asked suddenly.

Mirela was again consulting her phone. "Yes, sunshine. We saw the fire truck, do you not remember? And I saw people leaving when I called Margo."

Of course it was over. My mind was going, right before my eyes.

At least that would take a little pressure off the town; a lot of people came from the Cape itself just for the parade, and left when it was over. Not that it was going to quiet down by any stretch of the imagination. Tea Dance would be in full swing at the Boatslip; the bars would be overflowing with people already two-thirds of the way to drunk, while Commercial Street would be filled with people already well there; and I wasn't in the mood for any of it. "There's nowhere I really want to go," I said dubiously. "I don't think I can handle so many people."

"We will go to the inn," said Mirela decisively.

I didn't have the energy to argue. It was that or go home, where I could sit in my tiny apartment and listen to the backbeat from the club downstairs. And worry about Ali.

The inn was buzzing, but the downstairs bar, not being currently open, was quiet and blessedly cool; Glenn had installed three separate window air conditioners and they were whirring away. The lights were off; it felt like a protected place.

In one corner a group was clustered around one of the low tables—my faithful informal float committee. Deprived of their float and probably feeling left out of the parade celebrations, the five of them were probably commiserating.

I didn't join them. Somehow this morning's events seemed very far away. I'd lived a couple of lifetimes since then.

I went behind the bar and poured myself a tomato juice; Mirela flipped her hand when I asked her what she wanted. I took that to mean her usual, which was gin and tonic, and I inexpertly mixed one, added ice and lime, and went over to the other side of the bar and hopped up on a stool beside her. "Cheers." I drank tomato juice. "How do we know when the attorney gets here?"

"She will text when she is close," said Mirela. "Do not worry, sunshine. She is very good. She will take care of Ali. I would trust her with anything. So you must not worry."

"Never in the history of worrying has telling someone not to worry worked," I said, wondering if I was being profound or simply getting loonier by the second. I held the cold glass to my forehead. "This is a nightmare."

"It is," said Mirela, with her usual gift for understatement, "one of the strangest Carnivals ever."

And about to get stranger, I thought. As if on cue, the door was shoved open and two very large men entered, intent on their conversation together.

Two very large men in military-style uniforms. Massachusetts state troopers. And how they managed to even breathe in this heat dressed like Hitler's auxiliaries was beyond my understanding.

"Oh, joy," I said.

One of them—Trooper Ben Gerace, I thought—heard me. "Ms. Riley. The manager said we could find you here."

"Trooper Gerace."

Mirela was looking interested. I made half-hearted introductions. "What can I do for you?" I had a feeling that, whatever it was, I wasn't going to like it.

"Offer them a drink," Mirela suggested. Gerace looked like he'd be happy to accept. He also was giving Mirela an up-and-down inspection, everything but signaling his intent.

Mel Harvey gave me a look in which I read a faint apology. "Sorry to intrude on you, Ms. Riley. We're helping with the investigation."

I didn't have to ask which one. We'd passed seamlessly from the float to Ali. "Yes, I remember," I said. Even our previous encounter felt like it had happened eons ago. "We just met one of your friends over at the police station," I said.

Harvey nodded. "Detective Captain Norton," he said.

"Unpleasant man," I added.

"Do you live in Provincetown?" Gerace was asking Mirela. Wait, was he *flirting* with her? I started to say something, but Trooper Harvey managed to catch my attention in time. Just as well. "I'm sorry for your troubles," he said.

"Thank you." I paused. "Did you say you were working with that detective?"

"Temporarily." He seemed to check internally to see what was okay to share with a civilian. "We don't work out of the same barracks. It's just, we happened to already be here."

"On the spot," I agreed.

There was an awkward pause. Mirela was saying something but I wasn't paying attention. I cleared my throat. "I don't suppose there's anything you can tell me," I ventured.

"It's your friend who was taken into custody?"

I nodded. Taken into custody. Ali. How on earth did those two go together? "It's stupid," I said. "Ali—he's one of the good guys, you know—one of you, come to that. Law enforcement. He works for Immigration and Customs Enforcement." I swallowed. Something about being around these people had me talking like them. "I'd think that would mean you could cut him a break."

If anything, he stiffened still more in his uniform. "No one is above the law," he said.

"No, of course not." I turned back gloomily to my tomato juice.

"For what it's worth, ma'am," he said seriously, "I'm sure he will be treated well. You don't have to worry about that."

"Kind of you," I managed. I was seriously close to tears again. Ali. In jail. It was unthinkable. I swallowed again. "You were looking for me?"

"Excuse me?"

"When you came in here. You were looking for me?"

"Right." His eyes drilled into his partner's back—if indeed they were partners, I had no idea how things worked in the state police—and as if by osmosis Trooper Gerace turned around. Mirela looked faintly amused; it takes a lot more than a man in uniform hitting on her to be perturbing.

"We've been doing a reconstruction of the explosion this morning," said Trooper Harvey. "And I just wanted to confirm you told—um—" he pulled out a small notebook from his pocket, flipped a few pages, consulted it— "you told your manager, and the inn's owner, and someone called Mr. Steers, that you'd be going out to inspect the float first thing this morning."

"It wasn't a secret," I said defensively.

"And you also told Agent Hakim and Commissioner Hakim," he said. I liked him for using Ali's title.

I gestured helplessly. "At some point, yeah, I'm sure I did. This is insane. It's not just Ali wouldn't do this at all, he certainly is the *last* person who would do anything to hurt me!"

"So," said Trooper Gerace, "who would be the *first* person?"

***

It took Attorney Margo Nash nearly three hours to get to Provincetown; the Technicolor sunset was performing its gaudy light show in the sky by the time Mirela got the lawyer's text and we headed back to the police station to meet her.

She was brisk and no-nonsense, and as fresh as if she'd stepped out of her shower instead of having spent the past three hours in summer traffic. I wondered how she did it; for my part, I felt like a limp dishrag. Then again, I'd had a day of it, and it wasn't close to being over. "What do I need to know here?"

"He didn't do anything," I said.

She looked at me sharply. "That isn't helpful," she said, and turned to Mirela. "What?"

"I think," said Mirela slowly, "they are going to invoke national security."

It was my turn for a sharp look. "You didn't tell me that."

"I did not wish to worry you more than you already are worried," she said, looking unhappy.

"In that case," said Margo, "we may have a problem. All right." She rapped on the bulletproof Plexiglass separating us from the dispatcher. "I'd like to see my client now," she said.

It took them another ten minutes to usher Margo back into wherever it was they were holding Ali, and I already had worn a groove in the linoleum from pacing. "You need to stop now," Mirela told me twice; I ignored her both times. National security, I was thinking. Of course they'd go for national security. What else had I expected?

For the first time, it dawned on me, viscerally, that this might not end well. As in, really. That Ali might not be coming home with me. That this could get really serious really quickly. "This isn't happening," I said to Mirela for about the hundredth time.

"Do not go ahead of where we are, sunshine," she said. "We need to wait to see what Margo has to say."

"She's not getting him out tonight," I said. There was nothing in the world I wanted more than for her to get him out tonight.

"No," Mirela acknowledged. "She is not getting him out tonight."

When Margo finally emerged, to my surprise, Karen was with her. I took one look at their faces and knew. "What is it? What's happened?"

"Is there someplace quieter we can go?" asked Margo. It was perfectly quiet at the police station; her meaning was clear. "Not during Carnival," I said, my brain running down the various options. Back to the inn, yet again? To my apartment?

Mirela said calmly, "We need to walk a dog."

We all stared at her, and then I nodded. "Not many people at the dog park this time of night," I said.

"And it is close by," said Mirela. She was brilliant. I wanted to hug her, but if I had, I'd have started crying. As it was, I was pretty close to breaking down. I was doing the best I could to hang onto whatever shreds of sanity were left. I could probably count them.

No one said anything until we let ourselves in through the gate. No one was there, no little dogs yapping and running in frenzied circles, no large hulking dogs trying to lick us to death. I have to be forgiven my assumptions: I'm a cat person living in a dog town.

And it was still hot as hell.

Margo was direct; she may have been thinking about the three hours on the road she still had ahead of her. "He hasn't yet been charged," she said. "But he probably will be. They can hold him until then."

Karen had gotten more information than Margo. Criminal lawyers were the enemy; a police commissioner was family. Even if she was actually family to the accused; that came second. The blue line always came first. "I believe tomorrow he may be charged under the Patriot Act," she said. Her voice was steady.

There were a million things to say to that. I didn't say any of them.

Karen went on, "The device on the float was a very small pipe bomb. It's probable it wasn't meant to do much harm. Maybe exactly what it did, mess up your artwork. If it had gone off later, it might have caused a significant disruption in the parade. It's doubtful anyone would have been killed."

I didn't know why in hell anyone would want to plant a non-lethal pipe bomb, but I was beyond caring. "So what's the problem?" I demanded.

"What was inside, is the problem," she said. "Usually, you understand, pipe bombs are filled with shrapnel—nails, stuff like that, anything that will cause maximum harm, maximum damage."

I didn't say anything. Mirela moistened her lips. "And?" she asked.

"The only thing inside the PVC pipe on the float was powder," she said.

"What kind of powder?" I was sure I already knew.

"Talcum," she said.

We all stared at her. I was feeling like I'd left my brain in bed when I got up that morning. "Wait—"

Margo said, impatiently, "A trial run. Bioterrorism." This was a woman who got straight to the point.

Karen nodded. "To see if it worked as planned."

"It didn't," I said. "It went off early."

Karen nodded. "Exactly the kind of error a trial run takes care of," she said.

"And, what? They grabbed Ali because...?"

Karen looked at me calmly. "There was more of it in his luggage," she said.

"They can't know that! His suitcase is in my apartment! They can't have..." My voice trailed off. Of course they had.

"That's why the Patriot Act. There's no need for a search warrant." She paused. "They have been to the inn as well."

"Who? Who, exactly?"

"The state police," she said. "Acting for the FBI. One of the special agents in charge will be here tomorrow from the Boston office and will cover everything then. There's a lot of interagency one-upmanship going on here." She was sounding more like the commissioner and less like Karen; maybe it was because we were now in her professional world, or maybe it was just easier than seeing all this as his sister. Of course, the only reason she knew any of this was because she was police commissioner. Professional courtesy, ma'am. When we haul your baby brother in as a terrorist, we'll be sure to tell you why.

I was still assimilating what seemed like violations on top of violations. I wondered which of the troopers, Gerace or Harvey, had gone through my apartment. Tweedledum and Tweedledee, take your pick. Or Morton-Norton-Whatever. It could have been Norton. That's where I'd put my money, anyway. Where had they looked? Had they gone through my underwear drawer? Had they touched my *cat*?

I tried one last time. "But Ali works for the government. They can't treat him like this. Why isn't ICE involved? They'd take care of him, wouldn't they?"

Mirela reached over and took my hand. I shook her off.

Margo said, her voice even, "It's going to get very complicated from here on in, with so many agencies potentially involved. The best thing everyone can do tonight is get some rest. Tomorrow is going to be difficult enough."

I turned to her. She had talked to Ali. "What did he tell you? What did he say?"

239

"What I can tell you," she said, carefully, "is he is maintaining his innocence, and that's what I intend to prove. I'm sorry. Anything beyond that is privileged."

Yeah, yeah, yeah. *Breathe, Riley,* I reminded myself. *Just breathe. This, too, shall pass.*

But I really had no idea how.

16

Margo went home. Mirela went home. Commercial Street was in full swing, with costumed revelers reeling around, three deep, singing and yelling. It was as though they were moving about in a parallel universe. How could they just walk around as if nothing had happened?

Karen said, abruptly, "Do you need to sleep now?"

Sleep? What was that? "I probably *can't* sleep now," I said. "Why, what's the alternative?"

"Come back with me. There are some things I can tell you."

I was starting to wonder why I'd ever felt uncomfortable around Karen. If you'd asked me a month before whether we'd ever be this close, I'd have said if so, somewhere up in the stratosphere, pigs would be flying. "Okay," I said. "Yes. Thanks. I'd appreciate that."

We didn't say much else. She seemed deep in thought. Her headscarf was tied so tightly it hadn't moved throughout her day, but there was a sweat stain on her dress and everything looked pretty wrinkled. She must be, I thought, at least as tired as I was. I might have begun my day earlier, and with a very big proverbial bang; but she'd been in that police station for a whole lot of hours.

I waved my hand halfheartedly at the kid at the front desk and yet again couldn't remember his name. I wasn't even positive at this point I could remember *my* name. We didn't say anything until we were upstairs in her suite, with the door shut firmly behind us. Karen waved me over to the efficiency kitchen. "Help yourself," she said. "I'll be right back."

She disappeared into the bedroom, and I explored the refrigerator. What I really wanted was a Scotch the size of Chicago, but that wasn't going to help me and would surely offend her. I settled for orange juice. At least it was cold.

Karen came back out, dressed in jeans and a t-shirt and minus the headscarf, her long glossy black hair swinging free around her face. "Orange juice?" I offered and she nodded, tossing herself onto the sofa, rubbing her forehead. "I think," she said, "it is time I told you something."

I handed her the glass and took a seat in one of the armchairs across from her. "Okay," I said, a little guardedly. At least now I was going to know. The monster that had been flexing its muscles in the undercurrents of Ali and Karen's interactions was going to surface. Whatever it was, I'd rather know what it looked like.

She drank some orange juice, thirstily, and set the glass on the coffee table. "It was not an accident I came to Provincetown for my vacation," she said.

"Okay," I said again, not sure how to respond, my voice halfway between a comment and a question. I'd already worked that much out.

"You probably wouldn't know this," she said, "but the Department of Homeland Security has quietly closed down its domestic terrorism unit." She looked at me, took a deep breath. "Apparently there is no more domestic terrorism," she said, calmly, her voice level. Not inviting outrage.

I stared at her. It seemed there wasn't a week anymore when someone didn't walk into a church or a mosque or a synagogue and shoot a whole bunch of people. And that's not even counting the school and concert shootings. What kind of terrorists were they? "The lone wolf syndrome?" I said, having paid attention to the news.

Karen nodded. "That's the way it's being framed," she agreed. "One crazy person with a gun, and no need to view it as an epidemic. Which, of course, it is. But not part of the current narrative." She sighed, a lost sound. "Many of us in local law enforcement have been very concerned about the closure. Not just what it means for the country as a whole— and of course it means a great deal for the country as a whole—but also for our ability to respond to these events when they take place in our communities."

No one, I noticed, was suggesting they wouldn't continue to take place. And that was perhaps the saddest part of all.

"Some of us have been attempting to step up our own ability to monitor the possibility of domestic terrorism in our own jurisdictions and see if we cannot do something to derail future attacks."

"And that brought you to *Provincetown?*" It didn't make sense. People didn't lock their doors here. When a house burned down, we held fundraisers to help the people get back on their feet. Our worst crime is bicycle theft.

She leaned forward, picked up her glass, drained it, set it down again. "There is a group called Brigade America," she said. There was no emotional inflection in her voice. "Their tagline is *you're our better America.* According to the Southern Poverty Law Center, it's the largest anti-Muslim group in America. It pushes wild anti-Muslim conspiracy theories, denigrates American Muslims, and deliberately conflates mainstream and radical Islam. But it does much more: it's also anti-immigration, anti-gay, and clearly white supremacist."

"An equal-opportunity hate group," I murmured.

She nodded. "The group has attracted a lot of far-right extremists," she said. "White supremacists, neo-Nazis, fascists, militia group members. People on the fringes, for whom Brigade America isn't hateful enough. They think it doesn't go far enough. There have been a number of demonstrations and events that attract anti-government extremists—and they came with rifles and riot gear. One of those extremist groups, the White Rebels, claimed a member of one of Brigade America asked them to assist with security, to help defend free speech."

I frowned. "The White Rebels?"

She flipped her hand. "It doesn't matter. They all have different names; they all believe in the same things. They chanted in Charlottesville. They bomb churches. They shoot people in synagogues. The White Rebels is just one group, but a powerful one, one of the largest radical antigovernment groups in the United States." She shrugged. "It doesn't matter," she said again. "The names don't matter. The hatred does." She took a deep breath. "So over the past eight to ten months, I've been monitoring Brigade America. They have an active Boston chapter, and it's up to me to keep my city safe."

"How do you do that? Did you send someone undercover?"

She looked, of all things, vaguely amused. "Sydney, I have no budget for that. The domestic terrorism unit did, and was doing some excellent work when the federal government cut it off. No: when I say monitor, it's exactly what I mean. Listen in, if you prefer. Have you ever heard of DarkChan?"

I shook my head.

"It stands for Dark Channel. It's the closest ordinary people can get to the dark web, the illegal stuff." She sighed. "It's a completely unmoderated message-board site where right-wing extremists gather to exchange a very limited set of views, share conspiracy theories, and egg each other on. They have conversations they refer to as jokes, jokes that denigrate every possible minority group. The Christchurch mosque shooter, the California synagogue shooter, both were radicalized there and posted their manifestos on the site. There's no reason to believe it won't continue to flourish and continue to support violence."

"Why doesn't it get closed down?"

She shrugged again, and seeing her glass empty, got up and went to pour orange juice. "More?"

"I'm good, thanks."

She came back to the sofa. "There are a lot of first-amendment concerns," she said. "But here's the problem: if you keep joking about something like this long enough, eventually somebody is going to do it for real. They say they're joking when they admire the Nazis, but the truth is they're not: they want the country to collapse into a civil war so white nationalist murder gangs can execute everyone who's not Aryan. A race war."

It sounded way too apocalyptic for a summer night in P'town. Then again, my float had blown up, and that wasn't exactly a common occurrence here, either. I shivered. "And your group—America's Brigade—it's part of this site?"

"Brigade America," she corrected. "And, yeah, the group uses DarkChan for sharing what it's doing, for getting ideas, that sort of thing. In many ways, it's less radical than the more radical elements on DarkChan, but it's just as deadly, because one of its stated goals is education. In other words, brainwashing." She took a deep breath. "Over the past four months there has been an uptick in conversations with the Cape Cod chapter."

"Wait—there's a Cape Cod chapter? There's a hate group *here*?"

She looked at me with pity. "Sydney— there's a hate group everywhere."

I remembered, then, the girl in the head-scarf at the office-supply store in Orleans. We weren't immune. No place, I realized belatedly, was immune. "But honestly, Karen—this isn't exactly the center of the universe. No one pays attention to what goes on here. Why would they waste their time on the Cape?"

"It turns out," said Karen, "the local chapter, and some of its affiliates, feel that's a problem."

I stared at her. "That makes no sense at all."

"Of course it does," she said. "Nothing happens here, right? So what if something did? It would shock the nation." She paused. "And what if they could point out that they've been right all the time, about Muslims, about gay people, about minorities and immigrants and all the people they hate... There is a need for education." It was clear the word was in quotation marks. "White liberals are giving the farm away to minorities and need to be radicalized. They need to know who the enemy is. They need to be *taught* who the enemy is."

I was starting to have a very bad feeling, something cold in the pit of my stomach. "Foreign Lands," I said softly. "The Carnival theme."

She nodded. "Foreign Lands," she confirmed. "What better theme for a parade in a town filled with people they already despise? It was very definitely viewed as a teaching moment, at least as far as we could tell." She drank some orange juice; my mouth was suddenly feeling dry and I wished I'd asked her for a refill, too. "We alerted the local police, of course, but they're always alert around Carnival time. And we didn't have anything specific to watch out for—not yet. But Ali was already planning to be here. Partly for vacation, partly to keep an eye on you."

"Wait, though," I objected. "They couldn't have known he'd be here, or especially not that *you'd* be here. They were planning all this anyway?"

Karen nodded. "They were originally planning to blame someone from the gay community," she said. "It didn't really matter who. Our presence here, as Muslims? They saw that as a gift. Frosting on the cake."

I couldn't contain myself any longer. "You *knew*," I said, watching her. "You knew this was going to happen. You knew they were going to set Ali up."

"We knew," she agreed calmly.

"And you told the police."

"We did."

I took a deep breath. The cold fist in my stomach was working overtime; I felt as though I'd been punched. "And you didn't tell me."

There was a moment of silence, taut and still, the seconds spinning out across the gulf I suddenly saw opening up between us, her watching me with nothing but concern on her face, and me thinking, *so this is the way it ends.*

"You know," said Karen, "there are a lot of platitudes I could feed you here. I will show you respect and not talk about any of them. Ali was uncomfortable with not telling you; you should know that, at least."

"I suppose that means I should thank you!"

She shrugged. "Thank me, don't thank me, it doesn't matter. We have some experience at this, Ali and I. Neither of us is here in an official capacity. There is no official capacity anymore: I told you, the feds closed the domestic terrorism unit."

"All the more reason, it seems to me, that I should know. You came to my town. Hell, Ali and I are a couple! It didn't occur to either of you I might, I don't know, *worry* a little when he got arrested?" Another thought dawned. "What was *that* about, anyway?"

"There's another layer to all this," she said calmly. "I haven't finished. Some of the participants on DarkChan belong to the law enforcement community."

I stared at her. "Where? Who? Not here in P'town?" *Julie?*

She shook her head. "Not as far as I know," she said, a little cautiously. "But white

251

supremacy has always been an attractive concept to many of the same people who are attracted to law enforcement. Back in the sixties, it wasn't unusual for a local chief of police to be part of the Ku Klux Klan."

"Someone in Boston?" That had to hurt; these were her people, her second family.

"No doubt some Boston police officers are white supremacists," she said. She seemed to be dealing with it well; I supposed she'd had plenty of time to get used to the idea. She'd been a cop for a lot of years. "But the messages we were tracking appeared to be coming out of the state police."

"I knew it!" I perked up. "That guy Norton!"

She was watching me. "Very possibly," she said.

"So that's it!" The synapses were fizzing again; I forgot how tired I was. "Karen! He's behind that guy running for sheriff in Barnstable—Thomas, Clark Thomas! And *he's* running on an anti-immigration platform! What better way to get the law-and-order vote than to have something stirred up, something bad happen?" Good Old Boy Clark, with his established reputation, bringing his brand of hatred down to the Cape. Someone who was saying the quiet parts out loud; white supremacists must love him. "So, the bomb? What was that?"

She sighed. "Every movement has its fringe elements," she said. "And they can be hard to control. I think—we think—this one's been freelancing. But the freelancing might be worse than the main movement." A breath, then, "We knew they were making a bomb," she said calmly. "We didn't know where they were going to detonate it, or how many people could be hurt or killed. We had to contain it, be able to do something about it." She took a deep breath. "Listen, Ali knew we were making ourselves targets, we knew they'd be paying attention when a couple of Muslims showed up for Carnival. So we used it to our advantage. We made sure they knew we were connected to the Race Point Inn, so we could be sure *that* was the float they were targeting."

"Thanks ever so much."

"I'm sorry you're taking this personally," she said. "The camera did catch Ali last night. He went to check out the device, to limit the harm. Turned out there wasn't much he had to do; just some damage to the electronic switches. He put a timer on it and made sure he was there when it went off, to keep people away from it."

Ali could work on a bomb? What else
didn't I know about him? I didn't have time to
assimilate it. "And it never occurred to either
of you—"

"Listen," she interrupted. "This isn't about
you. It isn't about us. It's a lot bigger than any
of us. What I told you at the dog park is true.
We hadn't known about the substance in the
pipe. We didn't know it was a trial run. And we
still don't know what the final target is."

"You don't even know *who* they are, do
you?" I asked. I'd slowed my emotions down a
little, enough to start thinking again instead of
just reacting. There was a shape starting to
coalesce in my mind, but I couldn't yet make it
out, not really.

"Specific names?" She shook her head.
"No. Everyone has a username online. But
we're monitoring what they're talking about.
There are several things going on here at
once." She obligingly ticked them off on her
fingers. "First. They wanted to disrupt the
Carnival parade. That's simply fun, at one level,
since a lot of people in the parade and a lot of
the people watching would be gay; but it also
lays the groundwork for saying the terrible
whomever is to blame. The terrible gays. The
terrible Jews. The terrible Muslims. Fill in the
blank." She drew in a deep breath. "Two: Ali's

presence—and mine, to some extent—was more than they could resist. Someone called the police station last night, said there was a Muslim terrorist in town and they'd better watch out. Three: it may or may not be the same people involved, but as I said, there was a secondary goal to the explosion—as a trial run for something bigger."

"In Boston," I said slowly. "Just like the Boston Marathon bombing."

"Not if I can help it," said Karen grimly. "This is different. If we're right about this, we're talking something much bigger and much more deadly, at the end of the day, than a bomb." She took a deep breath, spread her hands. "I don't think Clark Thomas or the state police know about this part of it. I think they just wanted to discredit any minority they could. But they've touched a very deep chord in someone, some more radical group, possibly someone aligned with neo-Nazis; there's been talk on DarkChan of contagion."

I stared at her. "Contagion." It wasn't even a question. We'd already passed that milestone. "But there wasn't a biological weapon on the float," I said.

"I told you: a trial run," said Karen with frightening certainty. "There will be, next time."

I thought about what would have happened if it hadn't been a trial run. If Ali and Karen hadn't been there. If something had been released on Commercial Street for the tens of thousands of people here for Carnival to breathe in. People would die; Carnival would be forever ruined; the town might never recover. My town. Along with my pain and self-pity, I could feel the first stirrings of anger. This *was* my town, damn it. They had no right.

Speaking of rights... "You still could have told me," I said suddenly, feeling the stab of pain again. "Did you think I couldn't be trusted?"

She sighed. "I am so sorry we felt we had to do it this way," she said. "If I were in your shoes, I'd be upset and angry, too. It wasn't an easy decision to make. And finally, we had to make the choice that would hurt you the least, even though it may not feel like that. It was for your own safety."

"My safety!" I really exploded then. "My *safety*? I thought it was someone trying to *kill* me! I thought they were trying to blow me up! And you let me think that, you and Ali. You didn't care."

"On the contrary, we care a great deal," said Karen softly. "We didn't have a choice. We had to look at the bigger picture, Sydney."

"So what really happened here?" I asked. I was starting to hit a wall, exhaustion and the after-effects of adrenaline taking over. "They were going to disrupt Carnival. You found out and came down. You made sure it was my float, and you made sure nobody got hurt. That doesn't explain why Ali's in jail."

"Ali's in jail because they think on their feet and they act quickly," she said. "The moment they knew he was in town, they shifted their focus. Instead of a gay person being blamed for your float—and believe me, they would have found someone to blame, and the more outrageous the person, the better— they shifted onto him. That's one of the reasons I know it's one of the offshoots of Brigade America. As soon as there was an overt Muslim in town, they went for him. They can't help themselves. It's their priority."

"And now?" I asked. "What happens now?"

"Now," she said, leaning forward, "we both get some rest, after all. Tomorrow may bring some surprises and we need to be ready for them."

17

D id you know," I said to Glenn the next morning, "the Patriot Act has nothing to do with patriots or patriotism?"

He was sitting at the empty bar, running down a list of something or other. "Didn't know that," he acknowledged without looking up

I balanced my cup of coffee on the edge of the bar and consulted my smartphone. "It's an acronym dreamed up by some twenty-something congressional staffer. No shit. Its real name is Uniting and Strengthening America by Providing Appropriate Tools Required to

Intercept and Obstruct Terrorism. Just trips right off the tongue, doesn't it?"

"Uh-huh." Then he looked up. "You're researching the Patriot Act?"

I nodded. "Picking up all sorts of interesting tidbits," I said. I was trying like hell to sound more chipper than I felt.

His gaze sharpened. "Is this about Ali?"

I shrugged; I had no idea what I was or wasn't supposed to know, what I could or couldn't share. "We're meeting with his attorney this morning," I said.

I hadn't slept particularly well. That surprised me, too. I'd been expecting to drop into bed and go out like a light, but even though my body was more than ready, my mind was of a different opinion. Ali. Danger. Bombs. Terrorists. White supremacists. Neo-fascists. Explosions.

Ibsen, with his usual uncanny ability to completely disregard whatever mood I was in, was being particularly annoying, walking back and forth across my chest and trying to lick my neck. I'd have closed him out of the bedroom if I'd had a bedroom. By the time I got home even the club downstairs had called it a night, and he was looking for a little excitement. Not getting it from me. I tossed and checked the time and tossed some more before finally giving in and taking half a sleeping pill. I woke up with a headache and the stirrings of panic in my gut.

Whatever had started wasn't over. Whatever wheels had been set in motion were on collision course with something. I hoped it wasn't me or anyone I cared for.

I skipped breakfast, fed Ibsen and attended to his litter box, then grabbed my bicycle and headed straight for the inn. The one thing about which I had any clarity was the only person here who had *any* idea what was going on was Karen.

But she was nowhere to be found when I arrived, which was why I'd ended up sitting in an empty bar with Glenn and reading about the Patriot Act on my tablet.

Glenn said, "They'll release him today." He sounded a lot surer than I felt. "It's typical. Like they used to blame the Irish immigrants for everything, or the Italians."

"That's not comforting," I said. "They killed Sacco and Vanzetti, didn't they?"

He looked at me blankly. "Are you trying to cheer yourself up?"

"I don't suppose I am." I looked glumly back at the tablet. There wasn't anything in the world that could cheer me up this morning. I jumped a couple of inches when my phone went off.

It was Mike. "Where are you?"

"In the front bar. Why?"

"You're not forgetting the wedding today, right?"

Oh, hell. Of course I was forgetting the wedding today. "Of course I'm not forgetting the wedding today," I said with as much indignation as I could muster. Was it really Friday already? I felt like I'd lived a few lifetimes and the week wasn't even over.

The wedding itself was simple enough, just the couple and a few of their friends, and they had reservations at the regular restaurant afterward, ordering off the menu, which meant I hadn't had to be in weeks of negotiation with Adrienne, our diva chef, or the maître d'. I had to have a portable speaker for the music out on the outside patio with the bower where we did weddings, and some champagne for a toast afterward, and all the little things that some-how need to be taken care of at the last minute, but by and large it wasn't going to require any heavy lifting.

The fact that I'd completely forgotten it, however, was more than a little concerning.

Glenn was watching me. "Someone else can see to it," he said gently. "You have a lot going on." Which was generous of him, since I'd managed to spend a fair amount of the inn's money on a float project that literally blew up in our faces and then spent the rest of the day AWOL and now wasn't doing the actual job for which I'd been hired.

"It's okay," I said. "I've got it." Or so I fervently hoped. I disconnected from Mike and pressed Karen's icon. Voicemail again. "Karen, it's Sydney. Did I miss you at the inn? I was hoping we could get together and..." I paused. Do what? Commiserate? Break Ali out of jail? "... anyway, give me a call when you get this message, okay? Thanks."

Glenn cleared his throat. "You know," he began, and then my phone buzzed. He motioned to me to answer it. "This is Sydney," I said.

"Yes," said the voice on the other end. "This is Margo Nash. I just got into town. Where is Karen?"

"I don't know," I said. "I'm only getting her voicemail."

"Me, too." The attorney was brisk. "I'm with Mirela at a place called Spindler's."

Right down the street. "I'll be there in five minutes," I said and disconnected the call. "Glenn—"

"Go," he said. "What time is the wedding?"

"Two-thirty. Plenty of time." Or so I hoped.

He nodded and made a shooing gesture. "Go."

I went.

Mirela and the attorney were upstairs on the deck overlooking Commercial Street and the East End bookshop. Margo was eating a bowl of yogurt, granola, and fruit; Mirela was drinking coffee and looking like she wanted a cigarette. I know the signs. "Hello, sunshine," Mirela said. "We are making plans."

"Is there any news?"

Margo patted her lips with a linen napkin. "How much did Commissioner Hakim tell you last night?" she asked.

I looked at her uneasily. "How do you know—"

"Let's not waste time," she said briskly. I had a feeling everything this woman did was brisk. "I want my client to be able to share a meal with you soon, instead of you watching me eat my breakfast, so let's just cut to the chase. We all know what's going on, and we need to work on a strategy for dealing with it. My priority is my client. Commissioner Hakim has other goals. It would be useful to know yours." She was looking at me.

I shifted uncomfortably in my chair. "I want Ali out of jail," I said. "But I also—Karen told me about a group with a chapter on Cape Cod—"

"Brigade America," supplied Mirela. I scowled at her. "You're well-informed," I said. I'd only learned of their existence last night. She shrugged and drank some more coffee.

"Good," said Margo unexpectedly. "Then I don't have to give you all the background."

"You know about them?" I asked. I was feeling increasingly bewildered. Margo had only come onto the scene yesterday, and she apparently was up to speed on everything going on. Had I been the last to know?

"How do you think I was spending my time at the police station yesterday?" she asked with some asperity. "Pay attention. We have a number of problems to solve."

A waiter approached the table, looking tentative. Margo waved him away. I could have done with some coffee, but it was pretty clear who was in charge here, and it wasn't me. "What separates real life from mystery novels," said Margo, "is real life gets messy. It's filled with intersecting story lines. And we're at one of those intersections."

Mirela said, "One line is the closing of the domestic terrorism unit in Homeland Security."

"How did you know that?"

She scowled at me. "It is not a secret. It is on their *website*, sunshine."

Margo waved to get our attention. "No squabbling, children," she said calmly. "And that is part of it. I believe my client and his sister arrived at the conclusion something was planned for Provincetown this week. They didn't know by whom."

I said, "Another line is DarkChan."

Margo nodded. "They used to hide behind hoods," she said. "Now they hide behind screens. You know Commissioner Hakim was investigating increased communication in Boston and on the Cape that traced back to a couple of specific Boston-based organizations and their communication with other hate groups on the message board." She caught my look. "My client gave me permission to talk about this."

"I was wondering why he hasn't talked to me about it," I said. I was starting to get a bad feeling again. Did Ali really think he couldn't trust me?

"He didn't want to scare you," said Margo.

"Never stopped him in the past."

She decided, probably sensibly, to ignore me. "There's been some evidence there's a political component to what's happening here. And certain elements within the state police are keeping a close eye on it."

Had she really said *certain elements within?* There were people who actually talked like that?

Margo was still speaking. "My client received some information implicating someone—he doesn't know who it is, or even if there's more than one individual—within the state police on Cape Cod, someone who was going to be involved in what this group, and I don't know what to call them, they're less organized than Brigade America but are definitely an offshoot of it, but he got wind it was going to happen here during Carnival."

"Wait," I said. "Ali's with ICE, not anybody's internal affairs unit."

She looked at me a little pityingly. "You don't think there's an immigration angle when you're dealing with an anti-Muslim hate group?"

"Not all Muslims are immigrants," I said. "Besides, he's in anti-trafficking."

"He's on loan," she said. "He—"

Mirela interrupted. "It does not matter, Sydney. You must not take this personally."

I stared at her. "How did *you* get so involved, anyway?" And how many more people were going to tell me not to take this personally? And why was I feeling like I was about to cry again?

"I am his friend," she said simply. "And Margo's."

"And yours," said Margo to me. "So pay attention. "Agent Hakim and Commissioner Hakim felt the best way to expose the neofascists inside the police—and let's not kid ourselves, that's precisely what they are—would be to bring them here."

"The explosion," I said slowly. "You're not saying he did that deliberately to—"

"Don't be ridiculous. He didn't do it at all. But once he discovered it, it seemed a terrific opportunity. Get arrested; all the Provincetown police will do is hold you for something like that. They'll refer it first to the Barnstable County District Attorney's office."

"I've met some of them," I said. This wasn't, after all, my first rodeo dealing with murder investigations on Cape Cod.

"And the DA's investigative arm is the state police," continued Margo, as though I hadn't said anything. "It would be interesting to know what strings were pulled in the selection of the investigators."

"That Morton guy," I said, nodding.

"Norton," she corrected me. "Don't get ahead of yourself here." She looked around. "Can we get the check?"

"Wait," I said. "Wait. So Ali found out about the explosion, made sure no one got hurt, and then got himself arrested for it so he could see which cops are white nationalists. What was his plan? It's not illegal to be a white nationalist."

Mirela had signaled the waiter, who appeared magically with the check. Mirela can do that; it's always impressed me. She passes the waiter test every time. She was signing the credit card slip and said, without looking up, "Is it not better to know who they are?"

"I still don't understand..." Margo was standing up, Mirela was standing up, and I was still completely bewildered. "Where are we going now?"

Margo looked at me as though I'd lost my mind. "To get Agent Hakim, of course."

We didn't have to wait long at the police station before Ali was produced. He didn't look the worse for wear. Karen was already with him, and she immediately grabbed Margo's arm and began to talk to her, fast and low.

Then he looked over and saw me.

18

There are certain undeniably awkward moments in life. The moment you criticize one friend to another in an email you then send to the wrong person. The moment you bring shepherd's pie and find out the potluck was vegetarian. The moment your mother sets you up with someone she thinks would be perfect husband material. (All three have happened to me, by the way. I lurch through life from one awkward moment to the next.)

None of them held a candle to the way I felt facing Ali.

I'd had time to think about this. I'd had time to feel the hurt, and now, no surprise, could feel it simmering into anger. He probably hadn't technically lied to me over the past couple of weeks, but he'd been keeping secrets for sure. Lies of omission? Is that a thing?

Margo was deep in conversation with Karen. No help there; no light banter to exchange to take the edge off the moment. Breathe, Riley; just breathe.

Ali wasn't helping. Ali wasn't saying anything. I took another deep breath. "What am I supposed to feel here?" I asked. "What am I supposed to say?"

He didn't pretend to misunderstand me, to ask me what I meant, to joke that I didn't look pleased to see him. That was Ali. He wouldn't ever insult me.

Except, of course, by his silence.

"I'm sorry you had to go through that," he said finally. "It wasn't my intention to hurt you."

"Heaven help me, then," I said, "when you really have a go at hurting me."

It didn't help that he was looking sexy as hell. He still hadn't shaved and had even more fashion-plate stubble on his chin, and his hair could have used a comb. He looked a little tough and a little determined and if I hadn't wanted to kill him so much I'd have wanted to jump on him.

Ali glanced over at his sister and attorney; they were arguing now, but quietly, probably because we were still standing right in front of the police station. He took a step closer to me. "Sydney, cara—"

"Don't cara me," I snapped. "And don't touch me, either. I can't believe you did this to me." Some small intelligent part of my brain was reminding me it wasn't actually all about me, but I never listen to that particular voice.

I also always regret not doing so. I'm a complicated creature.

"I was in danger, and you knew it, and you didn't tell me. You and Karen hatched up this plan together and decided to play me in order to implement it. I don't know about you, Ali, but in my world, people who love each other don't pull that kind of shit." Why didn't you tell me? Why?

He nodded; he'd been expecting this. "I don't blame you for being angry," he said quietly.

There was a pause while we both waited to see what would happen next. "Is that all?" I asked finally. "That's it? You don't blame me? Nothing about being sorry to have hurt me? Nothing about maybe you should have trusted me? You're just going to go all magnanimous and decide you don't blame me?"

Margo was looking at me; I guess I wasn't exactly whispering. Ali glanced at her and then looked back at me. "So what do we do now?" he asked.

I'd have said there was nothing he could do or say at that point to make me feel worse or to piss me off more than I already was, and then he went and said precisely that. "What the hell do you mean, what do we do now? I'm supposed to be the one to tell you what happens next? Make this all go away or be okay or some such shit? What am I, your mother?" I was yelling now and didn't care. "I don't know what you're doing now, but I'm going to work. And I really hope when I go home there won't be anything of yours in the apartment, because if there is, it's going out the window." I could feel myself hyperventilating slightly, and eased off. Breathe. I'd already made a fool of myself in front of God, the police, and the world; enough was enough. I closed my eyes. Breathe, Riley, breathe.

I was remembering our conversations when Ali first said Karen was coming down for Carnival. All the arguments about her being part of our lives for this week; how angry I'd been with him then. And none of it had been real. That was the worst part: none of it had been real. They'd always had this other purpose. Oh, we won't tell Sydney, that way it will all look more natural. She's not used to undercover operations; she might give us away.

I glared at Ali, then turned to the other two women, who were looking at me in a kind of shock. They knew. They'd known. Everybody in this little charade had known except for me. "Don't say anything!" I spat out at them. I turned back to Ali. "And don't you say anything, either," I said.

He didn't, which paradoxically and ridiculously made me even more angry. He couldn't stand up for himself? He couldn't stand up for us? "Fuck you," I said, and turned away to head up the street before the tears started.

I was still crying when the car slowed down beside me. "Get in," said Mike.

"Go away." I kept walking. We were on Shank Painter Road, the heat was almost unbearable, there was no shade anywhere, and his car had air-conditioning. Yep, I guess I am a masochist.

"Sydney!" The driver in the car behind Mike applied himself to his horn, and Mike cursed under his breath and pulled up quickly in front of me. The other car gave a final angry toot and accelerated fast to show us how important he was. Mike was already out of the car. "What's the matter with you?"

I said, "Why are you here? Did you follow us? Did you know all about it, too?"

"I have no idea what you're talking about," he said. "Know about what?"

"Why are you here?" I demanded again.

"I went to the Stop & Shop," he said slowly. He was looking worried. "What's wrong with you, Sydney?"

"It's not me!" I wailed, and to my absolute horror started crying afresh. Mike put an arm around my shoulder and guided to me the car, opening the passenger door and easing me inside. The residual cold air from when the car was running rushed to meet me.

He came around and got in behind the steering wheel but made no move to start the car again. "What is it, Sydney?"

"Ali," I managed to say before another wave of sobbing took over.

He nodded. "Have you been to see him? Is he all right?"

"He was always all right," I managed to say, and started taking deep breaths before I could cry any more. I had to get a grip. "Do you have a tissue?"

Of course he did. He produced a box from the back seat and I helped myself. Blew my nose a couple of times. Mike started the car and the rush of cold was bracing. "Thanks for stopping," I said, finally.

"What's going on?" His voice was gentle, undemanding, and I suddenly remembered the time when I'd first left home and was figuring out what it meant to be a grown-up and not doing especially well at it. My mother, for all her faults—and there are many, don't get me started—eased me through that period with grace and humor. I'd call up in a panic about something or other, not being able to breathe or crying and either way really unable to talk, and she'd sense it and chatter on for a few minutes, about inconsequential things, about nothing... my father had been up on a ladder doing something to the roof and nearly gave her a heart attack; the priest in their parish was doing a walk-a-thon; the garden was coming in beautifully... And then, when she sensed I was ready, she would say, "So tell me what's wrong," her voice gentle, and I'd tell her, and she'd help me figure out an answer to whatever it was. In that moment, Mike was my mother, that gentle undemanding voice, that assurance of support and love.

But I didn't want to cry again. "Karen didn't come here by accident," I said. "It was a setup. Or not a setup, really, but she and Ali have been tracking this neo-Nazi group, they knew there was going to be something happening here, and they told the police but not me..." Breathe. "And there's more to it than that, but Ali never told me any of it. They've been doing all these things on purpose and not telling me. He got arrested and didn't say it was part of their plan, he let me be scared and worried..."

I couldn't say any more. I was still processing the last twenty-four hours. We sat for a minute in something approximating silence, except I'd reached the hiccupping stage by then. "Well," said Mike at length, "that certainly sucks."

I looked at him and it all suddenly struck me as ridiculous. I managed a smile. "Yes," I agreed. "It certainly does."

He smiled back and reached over and squeezed my hand. "Want me to take you home?"

"God, no," I said. "I have a wedding in another hour and a half."

He raised his eyebrows. "Um, Sydney, no offense, but maybe you should go home first," he said. "You don't want to scare the couple completely out of their wits."

"Really?" I lowered the visor and peered at myself in the mirror. Raccoon eyes, smudges everywhere. Someday, someone will invent eye makeup that can stand up to serious hysterics. They'll make a fortune. "Yeah, I guess you'd better."

"Come on, then." He straightened himself in his seat and put on his seatbelt, waiting to pull into traffic. "Mike," I said in a very small voice.

"Yeah?"

"What if this means it's over? Me and Ali?"

"The only thing I can say is don't make any decisions now. You'll make a bad one. Everybody does when they get..."

"Hysterical?"

"I was going to say overwrought," he said and smiled. "But hysterical will do. Come on, let's go home."

But as we drove along Bradford and I looked out at all the gaiety—flags fluttering in front of guest houses, bicycles pedaling up the steep hills, people everywhere looking like they were having a good time—I wondered if what I was feeling was just the ache at the end of things.

***

The great thing about my profession, however frustrating and occasionally panic-ridden it can be, is it's totally absorbing. There's no way you can organize a wedding and think about anything besides the wedding.

I was standing next to the tiki bar out by the pool, waiting for the wedding party and officiant to arrive so I could guide them over to the bower-slash-gazebo (it's really a little of each) where we do weddings when Mirela appeared.

"Go away," I said. I'd managed somehow to get myself under control, had taken a quick rejuvenating shower, was dressed in my lightest summer-nothing dress, and could already feel the sweat trickling down my back. I liked that: it focused me on my discomfort rather than on fascists, exploding floats, and the potential end of my love life.

Mirela didn't go away. "You do not have the proper priorities," she said instead.

"When I need you to tell me how to live my life, I'll let you know," I said. I looked past her to where the photographer, Gregg Peterson, was arriving; that meant the rest of the party wouldn't be far behind. I smiled for Gregg, and said out of the corner of my mouth to Mirela, "Go away."

"I will wait until you are finished."

"No," I said, still not looking at her, still with my sunny smile in place. "You most certainly will not."

She didn't move. Now the officiant was coming in—Dianne, who would have done the float wedding, had it actually happened—and behind her I could see men in pale gray suits far too heavy for this weather. For one glorious second I considered pushing Mirela into the pool. It was tempting. I held the thought for another delicious moment and then moved forward past her, well away from temptation, and greeted Gregg and Dianne.

Mirela didn't take any of my hints. She stayed at the tiki bar drinking Diet Coke through the wedding ceremony, the toast afterward, the endless photographs. Finally when I couldn't put it off any longer I strolled over to her and hitched myself onto a stool. "So this is your plan? Follow me around all day?"

"Only until you listen to me."

I waved at the bartender. "A glass of ice, please, Alec." We didn't say anything until it arrived, and I immediately put the glass against first my forehead and then my neck. "I have never been this hot in my entire life."

"Sydney—" began Mirela, and I shook my head. "No," I said.

"You are being unkind," she pronounced.

"Me? My boyfriend lies to me for two weeks, and I'm the one being unkind? Don't talk to me, Mirela."

"You are pouting like a little girl."

"You try going through the week I've been going through, and see what it reduces you to."

She took my glass from me, set it on the bar, and, reaching over, swiveled my stool until I was facing her. "Listen to me, sunshine. This is not a game. There are horrible things happening in the world out there and all he wanted to do was keep those things from knocking at your door in your town."

"Then he made a complete—"

"I said to listen!" I'm not sure I'd ever seen Mirela this angry. "This is so much bigger than you and your small feelings. Do you not remember what these people stand for? What they want to go back to? Do you not read your own history? Terrible things have happened and still do and there is so much fear in this country now that anything could happen. And Ali is doing something constructive about it. Karen is doing something constructive about it. They are both very brave and they both risked their lives to be here and do this, and all you can see is your small feelings are hurt."

I stared at her. Not only had I never seen her this angry, I'd never heard this kind of monologue from her, either. And it didn't help things that the part of my brain that actually thinks things through was whispering she could be right.

I hate it when Mirela's right.

She wasn't finished with me. "And that is not all," she said. "It was down to Karen, the decision not to tell you. Ali wanted to, and she said no. She is accustomed to secrets, that one, and he agreed only on condition they could keep you safe. You know he would never have made that decision, him."

"I don't know that." But I did.

We sat for a moment in gloomy silence. She was right, of course; I was being petty and self-righteous and priggish and the thing was, I could probably sit here all day making a list of other relevant adjectives, but that wasn't getting any of us anywhere. I wondered where Ali was. I wondered what I could do to redeem myself.

There was only one thing to do. "We have to help them," I said.

Mirela shook her head. "No and no and no," she said. "You stay right out of it, sunshine. In case you did not notice, these are professionals. They know what they are doing."

"I've been able to figure things out in the past! Remember when Barry was killed—"

"Stop," she said. "You are not Miss Marple. You are not Hercule Poirot. You have been lucky to not be killed in the past. It is not a good idea to tempt fate any more than you already have done." She paused. "This is different, Sydney. These are people who want a war, not just a murder. It is out of your league. It is out of my league. It is a very bad idea."

"I've had very bad ideas before."

"And you have been fortunate when other people have rescued you from them."

That was true enough. Still... "Why are they still here?" I asked suddenly.

"What? Why are whom still here?"

"The bad guys." That's what they were, some unknown entity, amorphous and danger-ous. I couldn't visualize their faces. Unless it was Morton. I looked down at my hand, still bruised from my fall in the parking lot at the Harbor Hotel. Someone had done that. People who didn't even know me. I was collateral damage; I wasn't even the target.

Talk about feeling small.

But it didn't mean I couldn't do something. "There are three groups here," I said. "Proba-bly working together, but they're separate all the same."

"Sydney, do not do this." But she was listening, I knew she was listening, and I knew her little speech about not getting involved had been as much for her as it was for me.

I ticked them off on my fingers, much as Karen had done in her suite at the inn. Was it only last night? It felt like forever. "One, the stupid neo-Nazis, the ones that used the float as a dry run for something bigger, who want to make a point here because Provincetown is so opposite everything they believe in. Two, whoever is in the state police and giving them protection. And three, probably, Clark Thomas is behind at least some of this. And the way they all met and probably even coordinated everything was through that online message board, DarkChan."

She was nodding. Watching me. "You did this on purpose," I said slowly. "You knew once I came to my senses, I'd want to do something about it."

"Ali is on their radar," she said. "Karen is on their radar. Now my friend Margo is on their radar. But we are not."

"And yet, as you so subtly pointed out, we have no idea what we're doing. And stop playing me, Mirela."

"Then talk to Ali."

19

I called Ali. I watched the bridal party trickle out once the champagne was finished, and then I pressed his icon on my smartphone, wondering if he'd pick up, wondering what I'd say if he did.

"*Cara.*"

"It's Sydney," I said, stupidly: unless there were a lot of women he called *cara*, Ali had already identified my caller ID. "The one who loves you, three times over."

"I'm glad you called," he said simply.

"Me, too." I was acting like a sixteen-year-old inviting someone on a first date. There were rodents scrabbling around somewhere in my stomach. I gathered myself together. "Where are you?"

"I'm at the police station," he said calmly.

I gasped. "No, wait, they haven't—"

"No, they haven't," he agreed calmly. "We're sharing information."

"Not with Morton!"

"Norton," he corrected gently. "And no, not with him. But with you, if you'd like. Do you want to come over?"

"I'll be there as soon as I can."

I considered grabbing my bicycle, then thought about the crowds in the streets and backed off the idea. Walking was just fine. Fifteen very hot minutes later and I was looking through the Plexiglass again. "I'm here to see Agent Hakim," I said.

She buzzed me through without a word, and Ali was waiting on the other side of the door. Awkward Situation Number Two. He reached out his hand, and I took it, feeling his flesh warm against mine even in the frigid air-conditioning. Reassuring. Mildly erotic. "I'm sorry," I said again.

He squeezed my hand. "It's all good," he said. "Come on in and join the war council."

Karen and Julie and two guys I didn't know were in a conference room—not Norton's interview space, but in something more comfortable, with a coffee pot and cookies on the sideboard and magazines strewn about. "This is Sydney Riley," Ali announced to the table at large. He looked at me. "Special Agent Carlos Echevarria and Special Agent Donald Bond, from the FBI," he said. Both men nodded in my direction. Echevarria looked like a college professor in seersuckers and a marine sweater I was quite sure he had to remove when he went outside; Bond just looked like an FBI agent in a dark blue suit and white shirt. I nodded back and raised a hand in the direction of the two women. "Hey, Karen, hey, Julie."

"Why don't you sit down," said Julie. It wasn't a question.

Ali held out a chair for me and I sat. There was a pause, then Carlos Echevarria spoke. "The Boston office received an email yesterday. We haven't yet been able to trace its origins." He made it sound like they would at any second. I nodded. Busy day, yesterday. "The email," he said, "indicated we're supposed to keep an eye on Provincetown. Today."

"In what context?" I asked.

Ali answered. "What the email described was an *action*," he said. "It's typical terrorist language."

"There's a terrorist language?"

Donald Bond cleared his throat. "There have been studies," he said diffidently, "linking specific language, and I'm talking about value references, motive imagery, and integrative complexity, to a propensity to violent terrorist acts. When you compare them to the study's nonviolent comparison groups, the terrorist groups used more power, ingroup affiliation, and achievement motive imagery, and expressed lower levels of integrative complexity."

Wow. FBI-speak. I wasn't sure I knew exactly what his jargon all meant, but I got the general gist. "So you think this is a real threat?"

Everyone at the table, perhaps unconsciously, nodded. I did the same thing.

Julie said, "Then add a significantly increased state police presence in town," she said. "They generally leave by today—right after the parade, in fact, some of them. But not this year. That's no coincidence." I waited for her to say the detective's world-weary catchphrase *I don't believe in coincidences*, but she didn't.

"Norton?" I asked, pretty sure I had the name right this time. Now that he didn't scare me anymore, he was starting to be seriously irritating. "He seemed anxious to put the fear of God into all of us."

Karen shrugged. "It's unwise to try to narrow it to one person," she said. "This is a group effort."

"The thing is," I said, "you have to figure out what the email means. What the target is." It occurred to me maybe these career cops might just have already figured that out ahead of the wedding planner. "Sorry," I said quietly. "I just meant—"

"It's fine," said Ali. "Never be afraid to say anything. A fresh perspective is always useful." He drew in a deep breath. "Meanwhile, DarkChan is buzzing. Everyone's talking about watching Provincetown tonight. And they're getting lots of props for that—the homophobic world is alive and well, people saying they wish Provincetown would just break off and head out to sea, and—"

I interrupted him. "Tonight?" I said, startled. That was just a little too specific. I looked at Julie. "Tonight?"

She nodded. "We were just getting there," she said.

The vast amorphous monster I'd sensed before was on the move, slithering, coalescing into something more specific; the dragon was finally showing its scales.

Julie said, "There are fireworks tonight. They're set off from the end of MacMillan

Pier, right at the harbor. And only the end of it is closed off to the public; people can go out as far as the harbormaster's office. In fact, the pier itself gets crowded, and so do all the town beaches spreading out on either side of it." She sighed. "In fact, the whole of town."

"What are the chances," asked Echevarria, "of someone getting to the fireworks beforehand? Like sometime today?" He glanced at the other FBI agent. "I don't know much about fireworks," he said.

"They're handled responsibly," Julie said, bristling a little. "No one has access."

"Okay, but who could *get* access?" asked Karen.

"They're in a locked facility," said Julie. "It's not specially guarded. Our shifts check it out regularly. There's never been a problem. No one's ever tried to break in."

There was a silence around the table and I could almost sense everyone sharing the same thought. *There's a first time for everything...*

Echevarria stirred and said, "Our analyst thinks we're looking for three individuals. And if they're following the usual terrorist playbook, they won't be apart from each other at all in the time leading up to the attack."

That shouldn't be hard to spot, I thought dejectedly. Three guys in a town filled with groups of guys. *Be helpful, Riley.* "What kind of guys are we looking for?" I asked.

Beside me, Ali said, "*You're* not looking for anybody, Sydney."

"Of course I am," I said to him. "I know, I know, I'm not an expert here, but I can always tell you, or Julie, or Karen, if I see something untoward." I didn't know whether or not to include the FBI agents in my list.

I could see a gleam in Ali's eyes as he mouthed the word *untoward*, and knew I'd pay for it later. All he said, though, was, "All right. If that's *all* you do."

"The trouble is, no one bothers to describe themselves on DarkChan," complained Bond. "They'll post videos after the event, though even then sometimes, if they haven't gotten taken in, they'll disguise themselves or pixilate the images so no one knows who they are."

"So we have no idea who we're looking for," I said flatly.

Karen glanced at me. "They probably won't oblige us with t-shirts that say, *terrorist here, terrorist here!*" she said gently. I made a face at her. It said everything that I finally felt comfortable doing so.

"We're doing what we can to narrow it down," said Ali. "Meantime, everyone, the focus is on MacMillan Pier. There's no way anyone unauthorized should get any kind of access to those fireworks."

Bond nodded and stood up. "We're on it," he said.

"One more thing," said Julie, stopping him. "We want this to go quietly. This town is full of people who have been altering their states of consciousness for several days. I don't want to cause a panic. That could end up being more dangerous than anything your musketeers can dream up."

The agent nodded. "Understood," he said, and left the room. There was a small silence in his wake. "What are we doing about the state police angle?" asked Echevarria.

"Ali's working it," said Karen, briefly. I remembered Margo's assessment that having a number of agencies involved was going to complicate things, and realized she was right. Karen didn't want to give up her probe into the state police, not to the FBI, not to anyone. Ali ducked his head. "I'm on it," he agreed.

"You'll share when—"

"—I have data to share," Ali said firmly. Echevarria didn't like it, but there wasn't much he could say except maybe *liar, liar, pants on fire.* He nodded, stood up. "We'll be in touch," he said finally.

"Let's all check back in an hour," suggested Julie, and everyone nodded. Ali and I wandered outside together. "You have things to do," I said.

"Yeah, I'm afraid so."

"Good luck," I said. Or was it *happy hunting? Break a leg?* "I'll be at the inn."

"Great." He kissed my cheek, already anxious to be out there and into the fight. "See you soon."

With all the information I'd just received, I fervently hoped it wouldn't be at the hospital.

20

How can we find out where neo-Nazis are staying in town?" I asked Glenn. He looked shocked. "What neo-Nazis in town?"

"They're here," I told him. He was sitting by the pool drinking something creamy-white and frothy and watching some male guests swim, or at least pretend to. I'd plopped down on the chaise lounge next to his, facing him, elbows on knees, intent.

"Okay," he said slowly, drawing out the vowel. "And we know this how?"

"It's a long story." I reached over and took his glass from him and tried a sip. Piña colada.

Nice. I gave it back. "The thing is, they came to wreak havoc, essentially, and apparently they're still here, so whatever they had planned, it wasn't just our float."

"These are the people who destroyed my float?" I'd finally gotten his attention.

"Ali and Karen have been monitoring them," I said, putting quotation marks around the verb. "They're posting about what they're doing. Three of them. And they're still in town. They said to watch them. Like a kid on a tricycle. They can't do anything without an audience." I laced my fingers across my knees and leaned back. It was amazing how getting life straightened out with Ali had made me feel better. We could do this. "So I know they're here. But I don't know where they are, here."

"Destroyed my float," muttered Glenn. He'd probably be delighted to take all of them on bare-handed. Probably could, come to that.

"Everyone—everyone being various flavors of police, and the FBI—think they're going to do something tonight, at the fireworks," I said.

"And you don't think so?"

I stared at him. "Of course I think so," I said. "I just thought it would be helpful if I could find them before anything happens. Ali and Karen and the FBI are looking for them, but we're the ones know this town. And you, you especially, know everything going on in town." I paused. "Think about it, Glenn. Has anyone talked to you about anything bothering them? People who seem a little strange? Maybe are always on their phones?" Someone had to be constantly updating DarkChan.

"Give me a break, Sydney," said Glenn. "You've just described half the people here."

"True," I said on an exhale. I was really at a loss as to what to ask next. Glenn looked concerned. "Why don't you do something normal?" he suggested.

I looked at him blankly. "Like what? What's normal?"

"Your job?" he responded diffidently. "If you go do some wedding paperwork or make some calls—and don't tell me there aren't any, I know there always are—then it puts your dilemma on a back burner. Sometimes that's all it takes to find the answer."

"You don't have some ulterior motive?" I asked, suspicion in my voice.

"Such as?"

"I don't know, such as making sure I do actually do my job?"

He flapped a hand at me and reached for his frothy summer cocktail. "You do your job just fine, Sydney," he said.

I raised my eyebrows. "High praise indeed," I said drily.

"Don't wait around for anything effusive," he said. "It's not in my nature."

"Don't I know," I said with feeling and grinned. "Okay, off to get some work done."

"And back-burner cogitating," he reminded me.

"That, too." I headed in and slipped behind the reception desk to consult the calendar in my little cubbyhole. Not actually a lot going on; I was way too organized. Sunday's two weddings were all set to go, with another cake masterpiece promised from Angus. He was considering a windmill that turned with sparklers at the tips of the arms. Not my area of expertise for sure. In fact, I was a little at a loss. It felt as if I should be doing something, I just didn't know what that something might be.

As though my thoughts had echoed in the caverns of the kitchen and summoned one of its inhabitants, Philip appeared at the front desk. "It's a disaster!" he announced.

Pete at the front desk got a horrified look on his face and turned around to look at me. Okay, I'd asked for it. "What's going on?" I asked, standing up and joining him behind the reception desk.

Philip looked relieved. "Oh, Sydney, doll, good to see you. We're in dire straits, you have no idea. We've run out of parsley and the bitch goddess says she can't do dinner tonight without it. And I can't go to the Stop & Shop! Both the cars are out!"

I knew better than to question our diva chef, Adrienne. If she said she couldn't do dinner, she wasn't doing dinner. I could waste time trying to track down one of the cars to take Philip, or... "I'll do it," I said. "Write down what you need, I'll go get it."

"Doll, you are the best!" Philip exclaimed, sunny again. "That will absolutely save our lives!"

"Yeah, well, you owe me," I said, then remembered Philip dropping everything to take me to the Outer Cape. "Never mind. It's fine."

He scribbled something on a file card and handed it to me. "Okay," I said. "We who are about to die salute you." Getting to the grocery store, getting through the grocery store, getting back from the grocery store were all challenges. Talk about back-burner cogitation! Plus, the Little Green Car was parked safely in its space up at the Monument parking lot. I was looking at an hour and a half, easy.

All in a day's work here at the Race Point Inn.

I fought my way back to Bradford Street and walked up its hills, sweat tricking down my back and into my eyes, until I came to the driveway that wends its way down from the Monument, and with a final supreme push managed to get up it, too, though my legs were shaking slightly by the time I got to the top. The Little Green Car stood waiting, its windows up, its interior promising heatstroke. There were a whole lot of people milling about the parking lot, tourists paying their fee to Channing Wilroy at the little reception shack and looking for a place to park, other tourists coming down out of the museum and looking for their cars, too hot to look with much alacrity.

I'd have to get in and start it and crank up the air conditioning, I thought, and then get out again and wait for it to kick in before I got behind the driving wheel. It was just too much to ask.

I opened the door, fishing in my bag for the keys—I might not lock it, but in The Season I don't actually leave the keys *in* the car—when I was vaguely aware of someone coming up behind me, of movement, the still air stirring. And then there was a great cracking pain and a flash of bright light and, after that, nothing at all.

21

Reality came staggering back slowly and raggedly and, with it, pain.

I wasn't even sure I was me, much less where I was or what had happened to me. I tried to fight my way through the cobwebs that seemed to be all around me, and the pain, and eventually realized I was on a surprisingly cold floor, with my hands tied somehow behind my back.

That sounds like a logical, sequential ordering of thoughts, but mine were anything but orderly. The cold and the pain announced themselves first, then the discomfort of my arms stretched behind me, and then I think there was more unconsciousness for a while before I surfaced again to take more stock of my situation. My immediate conclusion was that being unconscious had been better.

There was some light, but not a lot, and incredibly the floor I was on and the walls around me were made of stone. Wait—I'd been kidnapped and taken to a medieval castle?

A voice nearby said, "Are you awake now?" and I jumped as far as my aching body could. It was familiar, that voice, warmth and turquoise waters and palm trees bending in a gentle breeze, and I tried to place it. I knew it. Or at least I thought I did.

I managed to speak on my third try. "I'm awake," I croaked.

"Good. I've been worried. I've been thinking you had a bad concussion."

Doctor's words, and then I had it. "Thea," I managed to rasp. My throat felt like the inside of an incinerator.

"It might help you to sit up, if you can," she said.

I looked around in my limited space and saw I was next to a wall. With some effort and very little grace, I managed to scoot over and press myself against it until I was sitting with my back against the stone. It was a good thing I was reasonably fit.

The first thing I did was look for Thea, and found her sitting cross-legged nearby, her arms similarly behind her back. "Where are we?" I asked. I was still dazed and my head felt like it might explode at any moment.

She smiled, but there wasn't any joy or warmth in it. "Don't you recognize it?" she asked. "The Monument. At the top."

"I don't understand," I said. "That doesn't make sense. No one can tie us up here. The staff would know. The tourists would know." I Was babbling and didn't care. "Why isn't anybody here? The Monument's open to the public."

"They closed it."

I shook my head and immediately regretted it; the pain was almost blinding. I took a breath and fought down the immediate nausea. "They know we're here," I said. "Someone always comes to the top before they lock up to make sure everyone's gone." I knew everyone who worked at the museum and Monument; no one would have left me up at the top, tied up or otherwise.

"Not when there's a state policeman telling them it's empty and there's something official going on," she said. Her voice sounded way too calm for what she was saying.

Hell. Ali and Karen had been right about the state police involvement. The thought brought me little comfort. Nothing was actually bringing me much comfort at the moment; my head hurt and I had a lot more questions than answers. I looked across at Thea. "What happened?" I asked. Even to my own ears, my voice sounded forlorn.

"To you? I don't know," she said. "You were here when they brought me up."

"Who? Who brought you up? How?"

I sensed rather than saw her shrug. "All I know is they're racist," she said.

You can say that again, I thought, as panic began to nibble at the edges of my consciousness. *Breathe, Riley, just breathe...* "What do you mean?" I asked.

"They came for me at the clinic," she said. "A man opened the back door, the one where the ambulances come, and came in and grabbed my arm. He said there was someone injured out there, I had to come right away." A breath. "So I did."

Of course she did. It seemed obvious the Bad Guys, whoever they were, depended significantly on the kindness of strangers. In Provincetown, that usually worked. It apparently had for them. "And then what happened?" And, as the thought occurred, "Did you recognize him?"

"I don't think I ever saw him before," she said.

"No uniform?" It was a forlorn hope.

She shook her head, and all I can say is it must have hurt her much less than it had when I'd tried the same maneuver. "No, I saw that one later," she said. "The one in uniform. But I saw he had a tattoo on his neck, the one who took me," she said. "A very small tattoo, very discreet. Like a—" She stopped.

"Like a what?"

She said, slowly, "Like a Celtic cross, but cut off at the bottom. Like a sun. I don't know what it means."

I didn't, either, but if she thought they were racist, at least we were on the Aryan fast track.

Thea was still talking. "They put me in a van—there were two of them—and put these cuffs on me then. It's a transportation van, not a van with seats, and I was on a very dirty floor. They talked all the way here. They called me the n-word. They talked about other people, too, fags and kikes and some words I didn't recognize. They must have their own specialized vocabulary."

"That's a lot of conversation for such a short ride."

"Not really," said Thea. "We came by way of Truro at least, maybe even Wellfleet. They talked about getting there on time. Right on time. They called it the tower. They drove for a long time on the highway. I think they were waiting for some signal from somebody."

"Probably," I agreed for no particular reason. I really had very little idea what was going on. "I think I know why I'm here, Thea, but I can't figure out why you are."

"They don't need a reason," Thea said. "I'm black. I've listened to them long enough to know that's all they need for a why." But she sounded distracted.

I considered the situation. If we were right, this was the terrorist group, the one inside the hate organization, the splinter let's-get-straight-to-the-violence group. They were alarmingly equal-opportunity when it came to hatred. Me they'd taken for leverage, I was pretty sure of that. It could be they'd gone off-script when they saw Thea, especially in her role as doctor. Like Ali and Karen, she was just too tempting a target.

"Okay," I said. "I'll tell you what we think is happening, and I really am so sorry you got involved. There are people in town—well, they're the ones who planted the bomb in my parade float, and this wasn't made public, but the explosion released some powder into the air. Harmless. But my sister-in-law thought it was a practice run. Then the FBI got involved, and, well, it turns out there's been talk on this racist message board of watching P'town tonight. So we figured it had to do with the fireworks."

"But why are the state police working with them?"

I frowned. "Wait. What did you see? Which police?"

"They were out there, talking." She jerked her head toward the outside viewing area, the parapet that ran around the Monument. "One was in uniform, and the two guys who took me, one of them with the tattoo. Said they'd closed the museum and the Monument, so everybody was safe."

I thought about it. For most of the climb, the Monument is made up of a series of ramps around the four sides of the tower. It's probably how they were able to get both of us up. Thea was lightweight, but I knew I wasn't, or so my scale would have me believe. Though the last time I'd weighed myself it had assured me I weighed eleven pounds, so what did it know, anyway?

I guessed it was good to have confirmation, but I'd have dearly liked to get it some other way.

"It's the fireworks," I said again, trying to hang onto one positive fact in this whole mess. They were probably up in the Monument so they could watch it happen. But what would they see? Just the brilliant shooting stars; the powder would be invisible. The people's reactions, though... not so much. But I wasn't going to think about that: Ali and Julie and Karen and the FBI would be there in time. They'd make sure it didn't happen. "It will be all right," I said out loud, as much to reassure myself as it was to reassure Thea.

"Well," said a voice from the doorway, "that's one opinion, anyway."

***

I twisted as far as I could to look at him. Young, handsome, clean-cut, with blond hair, blue eyes, and chiseled features. It might have been one of the guys behind me that day at the pizza place; I couldn't tell. They all sort of looked alike, now I thought of it. And he was *smiling*, damn it. "How are you doing, Sydney?"

"Just ducky," I said. "Thanks for the cuffs. I always wanted to try a little S&M up in the Monument."

"Sure you have," he said. "Can't say that I'm surprised. You'd do anything. Hang out with fags, sleep with an Arab."

"You left out the black doctor," I reminded him.

"She's got such a great sense of humor," he said over his shoulder, and a second later another young-Aryan clone appeared in the doorway. This one had red hair, but the same starched and wholly wholesome demeanor. Like a Mormon missionary. Like a trust-fund baby.

"Please," I said to the redhead, "join the party. Don't let me stand in your way."

"We won't," he said, and tapped the blond guy on the shoulder. "It's ready."

The blond went past him out onto the viewing platform. The redhead didn't spare us a glance before heading down the ramps to the base of the monument—and out. I rather envied him.

"They look so normal," I said to Thea.

"No," she said. "They look so white."

I digested that for a moment. I was learning a lot I really didn't want to know about

311

myself and my own prejudices here. I really hoped I lived long enough to benefit.

Not much time for philosophy now, though. I said to Thea, a little desperately, "I'm not so sure this is about the fireworks, after all." They'd shaken me up more than I'd let show.

She was pursuing her own line of thought. "Can you come over here?"

I didn't see the point, but maybe close proximity to another person was what she needed to remain calm. I inched my way clumsily across. "Well?"

She leaned in. "In the side pocket of my scrubs," she whispered. "Emergency pocket-knife."

I scrunched myself slowly over so my back—and hands—were next to her pocket, and there it was. I worked it out slowly and then couldn't figure out how to get the knife part out of the knife. "You couldn't have a switchblade, could you?" I muttered.

"For heaven's sake, Sydney, give it to me."

Well, she *was* a doctor, it was logical she'd know her away around a knife better than I did. Her fingers pulled it from mine and she did some things and before I knew it, she'd freed her wrists from the plastic ties. She massaged her wrists a little before cutting mine free. "Come on!" She'd barely moved when the state trooper appeared in the doorway to the viewing-platform. And how many people were out there, anyway?

It wasn't who I'd expected. Not Norton. Not even sleazy Gerace. It was Mel Harvey, the guy who had been so nice. Apologetic, even. He took one look at Thea standing close to him and started taking in a big breath, a prelude to a yell. I stepped forward, blocking his view of Thea. "Trooper Harvey? Fancy meeting you here."

His eyes came to me. "How did you get loose?"

"Never doubt the power of a girl with her trusty Swiss army knife," I said.

"You never said you had one." Thea was moving slowly, almost imperceptibly; I could feel her. Keep watching me, I thought. Just keep watching me. "What, you think I told you my deepest, darkest secrets?" I asked Harvey. "You were nice, you weren't *that* nice."

Thea was behind him now. He seemed impossibly big; she looked impossibly tiny and frail. I had to keep talking. "So you're in on all this, are you?" I asked rhetorically, hoping my voice sounded calmer than I felt. "You surprise me, Trooper Harvey. You seemed so level-headed."

She knew her physiology, that was for sure. She stepped forward and in one quick gesture had grabbed his neck and applied pressure to some mysterious part of it that looked to me like all the other parts. "Help me!" she hissed as she took his weight.

I help her ease him down. "Did you kill him?"

"Of course not. I'm a doctor. He's asleep."

"For how long?"

She lifted her shoulders. "Who knows? It's not an exact science. Come on, now, let's go!"

I'd had time to think. "You go," I said. "Grab someone's mobile. Call the police. Call the inn. Call the harbormaster, I think they're all down at the harbormaster's. Get help here." I met her eyes. I'd finally worked it out. "The bomb isn't at the wharf," I said, urgently. "It's up here. They're going to set it off during the fireworks, and it's going to get dark soon. Go!"

She didn't take any more urging, trotting down the first set of ramps. I sat back and took a deep breath. They'd started big, with the Carnival parade, and they'd promised the second act would be even better. What was more impressive than Carnival?

It had to be the Monument.

And of course that meant they'd planned from the beginning they would die, and me, and Thea. Well, probably a lot of the town would die, too, if they were releasing what Ali and Karen thought they'd be releasing; but the point was, they were becoming martyrs to the cause. Every movement needs martyrs, doesn't it? Something to start something bigger; the spark that would set off the race war.

It wasn't the happiest thought I'd ever had.

Two of them up here, I thought. The Ralph Lauren boy outside and Trooper Unconscious in here. I had to stall them, somehow, until help arrived. I crawled over and fastidiously clipped open his holster and removed his gun. I had no idea when he'd wake up, but I wasn't taking any chances. Too bad I didn't have one of his handy-dandy plastic ties on me.

One down, one to go.

My brain was coming fuzzily back online and I was starting to think the guy on the floor might be a better ally than he was an enemy. I prodded him with the tip of my Mary Jane. How did you wake someone up when they've gotten the right nerve pinched in just the right way? "Hey," I said urgently and ineffectually, "wake up! Trooper Harvey! Wake up!"

He was showing signs of life, anyway. There was movement under his eyelids. I scrunched back up against the wall, holding the gun in both my hands. I had no idea whether or not I could even hit a barn door with it, but there was no reason anyone else had to know that.

The blond guy chose that moment to check in on us. He took one look at the body on the floor and turned to me. I was ready for him, still sitting down, my wrists on my knees, steadying the gun as I pointed it at him. "Don't think about it," I said in a voice I hoped was dangerous and offhand, as though I held guns on people every day.

After the first moment of shock had passed, he looked, if anything, amused. "You shoot me, and Jerry hears it downstairs and detonates," he said. "You don't really want to rush that, now, do you?" Normal voice. Normal intonation. Someone who should be being groomed for boardrooms, not terror cells. The banality of evil. Someone had written about that, hadn't they?

Of course, Thea was right: my perspective was skewed. I thought he looked normal because he looked like me. I was vaguely aware if any of us lived through this, I wasn't going to be able to look at anyone the same again. Never think about inclusion—and exclusion— the same. Possibly not even look at Ali the same.

And if we didn't? If I died here tonight, what would I be a martyr to?

Wake up, I urged Harvey silently. *Wake up, wake up, wake up.*

And then, as if he'd been waiting for that signal, for just that magical moment, he did.

22

He was better at it than I'd been. His eyes opened and then he seemed suddenly and completely awake, alert, conscious of his surroundings. His hand went immediately to his holster. "I have it, if this is what you're looking for," I said, and waved the gun for a moment before aiming it back at the blond.

Trooper Harvey pushed himself into a sitting position and he and the kid exchanged a look I couldn't interpret. "You're just delaying the inevitable," he told me.

"Maybe it just feels inevitable to you," I said, "because it's so inevitable for him." I jerked my head in the kid's direction. "He'll end up dead anyway, if not tonight, then on some other night planting some other bomb."

The blond said, conversationally, "Shut up, cunt."

I ignored him. I concentrated on Harvey. "You really don't mind dying for this cause of yours?"

"To start the race war," said the blond.

"Oh, for God's sake," I said, and looked back at Harvey. "I wouldn't have thought you'd want to die tonight. You seem pretty human to me."

"I'm not dying tonight," said Harvey.

"Really?" I asked. "How do you figure that? The Monument's going down and so is everyone in it."

"Chad," said the trooper, "let's take care of this now so we can get the hell out of here."

Of course his name was Chad. Who would have thought anything else? Probably Chad Something the Third.

"*That's* what Chad told you?" I asked, hoping to inject just the right level of incredulity into my voice. "You think you're setting this up and getting out?"

Chad said, "Don't listen to her, Mel."

"Don't listen to me, Mel," I agreed. "But here's the thing, I don't think you planned on martyrdom tonight. I'm sure you're on the same page as the boys about the whole racist thing, but I don't think that's what this is about for you." I had his attention now, anyway. "This isn't really about bombs and poison for you, is it? It's about getting Clark Thomas elected sheriff for Barnstable county. Helping your boy get into office, and then expecting favors from him and reaping the rewards." *And where the hell were the people Thea was summoning? Or maybe she hadn't gotten that far, maybe the redhead had intercepted her... was she even now at the foot of the Monument, dead, or back in cuffs?*

"No way," said Harvey, shaking his head. "We've got masks. We're ready." But he was watching the kid again.

"Ask Chad, then," I urged him. "Ask him how committed he is to old Clark."

"He's committed," said Harvey. "We all are. Thomas is going to be the best thing for the Cape. He's gonna close all the ports, the places where the illegals are coming in. He's giving ICE the respect and assistance it deserves. He's gonna bring us back to law and order. When people respected the police." He took a breath that sounded steady enough to me. "When people were afraid of the police. Clark's taking us there. Right now he's mobilizing so he's ready with his reaction to tonight.

He's got the media on alert. He's warning everyone we can't trust the aliens, and he's gonna prove it."

"Over your dead body," I said. "Literally."

He licked his lips. "She's wrong," he said. His eyes were on me, but his remark was for Chad.

"Hell," said the kid, "it doesn't matter now. Where do you think we were gonna run to? There's no fuse, you don't have to be bomb squad to know that's old school, old man." Ouch, I thought, Harvey must have been around my own age. "We're staying right here. Make the bang, kill the town, go down in the history books."

Mega-points to Karen for knowing in advance. Karen seemed to be able to get into these guys' heads; I wished she'd been able to see her way up to the Monument. Releasing whatever substance it was—and did it really matter which one?—from the Monument, a metaphorical point as well as a literal one. Invisible, no smell, no taste. Disseminated via explosion from the highest point in town. These people might be evil and greedy, but no one was going to accuse them of being stupid. I was starting to feel vaguely nauseated. "You knew about the powder?" I asked Harvey.

"After we're gone," he said stubbornly. But he believed me; you could see it in his eyes.

Chad wasn't waiting for him to come completely around to our way of thinking. He moved, suddenly and explosively—as only someone fit and in their early twenties can—and grabbed me, pulling me up hard against him. The gun, as he'd probably foreseen, went clattering across the floor. He pulled me over to the edge, where the central rampways provided a drop of God only knew how many feet. And had me hard against the edge.

A door away downstairs slammed open and there were footsteps, running. And Ali's voice. "Sydney!"

"I'm up here!" I screamed, before Chad jerked me again, his arm around my ribcage, forcing the breath suddenly out of me. "Shut up!" he snarled. No worries there. For a few scary moments I couldn't get a breath, much less make a sound.

"You were going to kill me." It was Harvey's voice, steady and flat. He'd retrieved the gun and was pointing it at Chad. He had finally figured out his new best friends didn't really have his best interests at heart.

Unfortunately, since I was in front of Chad, that meant he was also pointing his gun at me.

"Never thought anything different," said Chad. *Keep him talking*, I willed Harvey: *just keep him talking.* The footsteps were pounding louder now and had changed as the tower segued from stairways to ramps. Not that I exactly want to be rescued like a damsel in distress—well, okay, fine, I'm lying, I'd be ecstatic to be rescued. And my own Dudley Do-Right was on his way up to me. Or so I hoped.

But there was still the pesky problem of that gun pointing at my chest. And I didn't think Harvey would give it a second's thought to fire through me to reach Chad. He'd made it clear he meant to kill me anyway, what with the explosion and the substance inside the pipe. I closed my eyes. Better not to see it coming.

Eyes closed, I could visualize the man standing behind me. Preppy khakis, a Ralph Lauren polo shirt, no socks, boat shoes.

Boat shoes.

Before he could sense the thought, I lifted my leg and drove my heel down on his foot, as hard as it could go, and at the same time I ducked. He screamed in pain—boat shoes don't offer a lot of protection—and let go of me altogether. I rolled away.

My rescue party had reached the floor below us and I could see them now: Ali, looking beautiful and dangerous in the dim interior lighting; and, behind him, uniforms: Julie in her dark blue, Gerace in his field gray. Norton brought up the rear. I saw them; they saw me. "I'm okay!" I yelled to Ali.

At the same time, Gerace yelled, too. "Mel! Put the gun down!"

He shouldered his way to the front of the queue on the ramp. "Mel," he said again, and his voice was gentler, quieter, dead calm. "This isn't going to help anything."

Just when I'd decided Harvey wasn't going to respond, he spoke. "You're wrong," he said. "It's gonna make me feel a whole lot better."

"It won't," said Gerace. "Come on, man, I'm your *partner*. I care about you. Don't do this."

"You think one killing's gonna make a difference when I go to court?... Back *off*!" he yelled suddenly as he caught Gerace moving stealthily up the ramp. He swung the gun in my direction, and I head Ali's quick breath intake. Me, I wasn't breathing at all.

"All right, all right, I'll stay here, it's okay," said Gerace, and the gun went back to pointing at Chad, who hadn't moved in the interim. Maybe I'd broken his foot. I rather hoped so.

I found I could breathe again, and did so.

Harvey was looking a little crazed by now. His eyes kept shifting nervously between Chad and Gerace, but his grip on the gun never wavered. I wondered if I could reach him before he shot me, and I decided that was a move that belonged in the movies, not real life. The experts had arrived, anyway. *Trained professionals, do not attempt this at home...* Light-headed, that's what I was. I made the most imperceptible of movements in the other direction, toward the ramp. Toward Ali.

Gerace said, "Listen, Mel, man, I just want to talk to you. We can figure this out together."

"Nothing to figure out."

"We're on the same side," said Gerace.

Harvey laughed, but there wasn't anything funny in his voice. "The same side? Who're you kidding? I'm the one who supported Clark from the start. I'm the one he turns to every time he has a problem. I'm the one who wants to do something about this goddamned country."

"We all want to do something," said Gerace soothingly.

"Well, watch this," said Harvey, and he shot Chad.

It echoed around the Monument like fire-crackers going off all around us. I may have screamed; I know I gasped. I hadn't exactly expected him to *not* shoot, but...

The kid's body had hardly even started to fall when Gerace moved on Harvey and Ali moved on me. Below us, Julie had her radio out. "Ambulance and bomb squad," she was saying. Norton screwed up his grand entrance by tripping on the final step and falling flat-out on the floor. I didn't care if he wasn't the bad guy; I still didn't like him.

Ali was running his hands all over me, searching for injuries. I had a weird sense of *déjà vu*; it seemed he was spending half of Carnival asking me if I'm okay. Only when he was satisfied did he take my face in his hands and kiss me. Gerace had his former partner in cuffs, Norton was dusting himself off.

"Everyone out!" yelled Julie. "We gotta get out of the way for the bomb squad to do their work."

My legs were shaking and I was going cold. Adrenaline and shock, two days in a row. Mirela was right: I was really going to need a vacation after all this. "Come on," said Ali, his arm around me, and we started down the ramps.

And that is the story of how Thea and I saved Provincetown.

23

We didn't go back to the police station: I put my foot down (not the one I'd used on Chad; it turns out, when you do that, you hurt yourself, too, who knew?) and Glenn let us all meet in his office at the inn, large enough to accommodate everyone, private enough for discretion, luxurious enough to help me feel coddled.

Julie, to my surprise, had been all for it. "There's no need to alarm anyone," she said. "A lot of strangers at the police station, someone's going to notice. But guests are coming and going at the inn. Glenn's a good guy."

She gave us a police cruiser and driver to take us there. "Thea?" I asked Ali as we sat in the back seat. I didn't know the driver; he was one of the summer cops and looked about thirteen. "Did she call? Is that how you knew where we were?"

"She called," he confirmed. "Grabbed a phone off the first person she saw on Bradford."

"Then where is she now?"

He shrugged, pulled me closer to him. "Didn't see. Julie will track her down. If nothing else, she needs to give a statement."

"She needs to be given a big round of applause, not getting her statement taken," I said. "I wouldn't be here without her." I shivered. "I think maybe nobody would."

"I," said Ali, "plan to express my gratitude suitably. A bottle of whatever she likes to drink. Tickets to the Red Sox. Anything, for saving you."

"I think she'd settle for a new knife," I said. "Where's Karen?"

He frowned. "What are you doing, geolocation?"

The adrenaline was seeping out and I was feeling exhausted. I just wanted it all wrapped up nicely, tied off with pretty ribbons. "She was right about a whole lot of this," I said. Just wondering why she wasn't here. You know, part of the rescue party."

"She was checking something out," said Ali. He was doing it again, looking like his brain was running through data, like he was doing sums in his head.

"What?"

He sighed and pulled out his phone, scrolling through some texts. "Okay. Here it is. Thinks she knows who's been giving the Brigade people info on Provincetown. Going to see about it, will catch us later."

He caught my look. "You said it yourself," he said. "Where would they stay? Who would tell them what targets to hit? Someone has to be on the ground. Here, in place." He glanced out the window; we were pulling over in front of the inn. "Don't worry. Karen's good. If she thinks she's found someone, she's probably found them. And she's probably being extra-careful. There are a lot of people on the street; she won't want anybody getting hurt. I'll just text her to meet us here when she's done."

I got out of the car while he fiddled with his phone. Something was bothering me, but I couldn't put my finger on it and my brain felt like the synapses were firing into molasses. We headed in.

Karen and Thea may have been missing, but the rest of the gang was certainly all there. Ali and me, three or four Provincetown cops, Norton and a whole bunch of people from the state police, and the politicians: the chair of the board of selectmen, the local legislator, with the governor apparently on his way as well. Julie arrived a few minutes after we did.

Glenn had sent in coffee and brandy, and I for one didn't waste any time making some inroads into the latter. Feel tired? Drink brandy. Feel ill? Drink brandy. I sipped and felt the warmth spread around inside, felt myself finally relaxing. Someone was shooting video of the room. There were a couple of subdued conversations going on. It was quiet and almost peaceful.

Ali was talking with the guys from the FBI and came over to join me where I'd taken up station on the loveseat. "What's wrong?" I asked.

He was texting again. "Karen's still not an-swering," he said. He must have been really worried; only fifteen minutes earlier he'd been telling me she was fine, she knew what she was doing.

I didn't know what to say. I couldn't deny that her absence was starting to feel ominous. Echevarria broke off his conversation with one of the other FBI types, came over, pulled up a chair. Ali glanced at him. "I can't remember," he said to the FBI agent. "What was the name of the shooter at that mosque in Oregon? Last fall sometime?"

Echevarria frowned. "Hunter, wasn't it? Evan Hunter?"

"Yeah," said Ali. "That was it. That's where I heard it before. Manifesto on Dark-Chan? Recorded the whole thing?"

Echevarria nodded. "Going on ten months now," he said. "Why?"

"Someone's using his name again. Same place."

I stirred. "Why does that matter?"

"Because," said Ali, "they're talking about Karen and Provincetown."

The spike of something jarring, a memory I couldn't quite place. I wished it would go away, that Karen would walk in, that we could have a nice quiet postmortem and end this day.

It wasn't that other things weren't wrapping up nicely; calls kept coming in. The bomb on the Monument had been duly defused, with a couple of military types on hand to deal with its extra contents, and the fireworks started just after we were all back at the inn; I wasn't so tired I wasn't startling every time there was a big bang, which was pretty much continuous for the first five minutes.

Provincetown was still in the full grip of Carnival, none of the people we passed aware of how close they'd come to disaster. "If we all knew, we'd never be able to function," I said to Ali. "All the assassinations that never happen, all the bombs that don't go off, all the plots that never come to fruition. They probably happen every day, don't they?"

He kissed me. "You don't want to know."

I shivered. I was pretty sure he was right.

We sat on one of Glenn's loveseats, Ali's arm around me, me nodding out drowsily on his shoulder. Norton, self-important as ever, sat behind the desk. The two FBI guys were in the client chairs, everyone else around the room, sitting in Glenn's generous armchairs, perched on the folding chairs with which he'd augmented the room's furniture. For the first time since I'd walked up High Pole Hill, I was conscious of the heat; it had taken a hell of a backseat to everything that had happened since.

"What about the death threats?" I asked Ali. "Was this it, or do we still have more fun to come?"

"Yours wasn't a threat," he said. "Someone trying to help."

"Who?" But he didn't answer, and I wondered if it might have been Gerace, suspicious of Harvey but not wanting to rock the boat.

The voices washed over me, everyone talking in turn, it seemed everyone had something to say—it was a sort of post-mortem that could have been a lot more mortem than it turned out to be—and at some point I tuned them out. The adrenaline high was gone, the funny taste back in my mouth, and all I really wanted to do was go to bed. With my cat. And my boyfriend. And sleep for about four months.

The door slammed open and Karen walked into the room. Slowly. Hesitantly. Not like someone in authority; like someone walking on eggshells. Or jelly. Her eyes sought out Ali. He was already half on his feet when Thea and Emma came in behind her.

Karen said one word. "Hostage."

She wasn't exaggerating. Emma had an arm around Thea's shoulders and was holding a very large gun—half machine-gun, half pistol—against her side. "Fuck," said someone in the room, very softly.

I hadn't seen anyone draw, but they all had their guns out. Hers was bigger.

Ali was on his feet, but was still standing next to the sofa. "Karen?"

She said, her voice absolutely steady, "Emma belongs to Brigade America. She came to Provincetown intentionally to set things up for Carnival, and she's been organizing everything from here."

Adrenaline was doing a number on me again, and it felt like my brain had kicked into high gear. All those people staying in the house, people Thea hadn't known. Friends of Emma's. she'd said. Nice looking white guys. Chad had probably been among them.

Ali's voice was just as calm as his sister's. "Emma," he said, almost conversationally, "seems it hasn't worked out the way you wanted it to. There's no reason for anyone else to get hurt now."

Emma kicked the door shut behind her. "I'd say there's still an opportunity here," she said.

"I told her the same thing," Karen said. "No one else needs to get hurt. I suggested she and I might go to the police station on our own."

"How did you know?" I didn't realize I was about to say anything until I'd said it. I wasn't even sure who the question was meant for.

Karen said, "The person posting on Dark-Chan identified herself as a woman," she said.

"And I'd recognized one of Emma's guests, someone at her party."

I remembered, then, her sudden departure. Checking it out. Maybe wanting to be wrong.

Thea said, suddenly, "The tattoo. Emma's tattoo. The guy on the Monument had the same one."

"Shut up!" Emma shook Thea's shoulder. "You don't get to talk."

Thea didn't get the message. "You were going to marry me," she said. "You met me on purpose and you brought me here on purpose. It was all a lie. You wanted me because no one would suspect someone with a black girl-friend."

"Shut *up!*"

I didn't know if it was a sore spot and Emma was feeling bad about using Thea, or if she just didn't want the distraction when she was holding a machine pistol against her ribs. But that reminded me of something. "You were going to be on that float," I said. "You rigged it to explode. Why would you do that?"

Her eyes rested on me. Briefly. In that room, I wasn't much of a threat. "We knew no one was getting out," she said. "It didn't matter."

I shivered. Like her boy up at the Monument, Emma had never had any illusions she'd walk out of this alive.

Julie said, "Emma. I guarantee someone in this room has already called for help. We all have phones. We all have codes. You don't have a chance."

"Doesn't matter anymore. I don't have a chance. You don't have a chance. And a lot of other people didn't have a chance, either" said Emma. "You saw to that."

"What did I do?" asked Julie, reasonable, conversational. As though they were chatting over coffee.

"You police," said Emma.

"She wanted to be in this room," said Karen. She still had her back to Emma; it was as though she were goading her. "She wanted to be in here with a machine pistol and a room full of cops."

"It won't help anything, Emma," said Ali. "Whatever you believe that brought you—"

"Shut *up*!" She was still in control but you could feel the rage in her, emanating out in waves. I wondered if they'd show up on a heat-map. "Whatever it was? Try Ruby Ridge!"

There was a pause. "Ruby Ridge was a long time ago," said Ali finally. "It had nothing to do with you. You weren't at the Weaver place. You probably weren't even born then."

The name didn't mean anything to me, but Emma looked like a jolt of electricity had just gone through her. "My father killed himself because of Ruby Ridge," she said. "Didn't want to wait for the FBI to come for him, too."

"But that's not why we're here, is it?" asked Ali. "We're here because of Evan Hunter."

"Her brother," said Karen.

The mosque shooter from Oregon Ali had been asking about, had been looking up. And Thea at the party, laughing about Emma's tattoo, talking about getting it in Portland when she was out visiting family.

"Shut up, bitch!" There was an edge in Emma's voice, now, and an echo of something, something sad and lonely and far-away.

And then Karen moved, sudden and fast, turning into Emma, with her fist out. The gun swung around from Thea, perhaps reflexively, as she shot at Karen. She missed.

But she didn't miss Ali.

Everything seemed to happen very quickly after that. Someone secured Emma and her weapon. The door opened and a whole lot of people came flooding in. Someone went to help Thea. It was all a blur around me; all I could do was press down on the spreading scarlet that used to be my boyfriend's chest. "Ali, you son of a bitch, don't you dare leave me." I was sobbing the words. The ambulance people were there, a thin blonde woman, brisk in her jumpsuit. "We'll take him from here, ma'am, you have to let go."

Her partner was already shouting for a backboard and pressing on the wound. "Ali? Is that your name?" The unnaturally loud and calm voice of people who respond to emergencies for a living. "Ali, you're doing just fine. Just breathe for me now. Stay with me, Ali, stay with me, just breathe."

Just breathe, Hakim, just breathe. Please, oh please, just breathe...

And then we were in the ambulance and they were attaching oxygen, running a line. The EMT's voice. "Ali? Stay with me, man, you're gonna be fine."

I didn't realize I was holding Ali's hand until it twitched in mine. I squeezed it and he squeezed back.

Three times.

Author's Note

It's both wonderful and difficult to write about a real place, especially when you write about murder and mayhem! I mean to *encourage* you to visit Provincetown, so do remember that while the background and context (and even a few of the people!) are real, the plot is wholly fictional.

I describe Provincetown as I—and Sydney— experience it, but was stymied by the Pilgrim Monument. I ended up being faithful to parts of its description but not to the top floor. So don't be disappointed when you climb it and don't see things as Sydney did! There is indeed a beautiful Octagon House in the west end of town; but I don't know the people who live there and have just bor- rowed the house for Thea and Emma to rent for a while. Finally, there are no fireworks on Carnival Friday, but hey, it's not a bad idea.

Just as Miss Marple's beloved St. Mary Mead and Jessica Fletcher's Cabot Cove are often rocked by dastardly doings for the sake of their resident sleuths, so too have I brought a taste of mystery to P'town. In reality, though, it's a very peaceful village. Sydney's right: our major crime is the theft of bicycles.

I like living in a place like that.

Jeannette de Beauvoir
Provincetown, Massachusetts
Summer, 2019

Acknowledgments

Many thanks to Arthur Mahoney of HomePort Press, officially the World's Best Publisher. He encourages, corrects, challenges and—best of all—laughs. I am so glad he and Sydney found each other, and allow me to be part of their world.

My thanks go as always to all the beautiful people of Provincetown, who generously allowed me to use so many of them in my books. Any errors in their portrayal are mine.

To those who contribute in myriad ways to the creation of a Sydney story: Colin Kegler, Carem Bennett, Dianne Kopser (featured here as her own self), Bob Allen, Mike Miller, Julie Knapp (see! Twisted made its way in!), Julie & Katy Blackburn, Michelle Crone, Anastasia Czarnecki, and Tony Rodrigues (for all the Portuguese food, and the laughter). Thanks to Deborah Karacozian, Nan Cinnater, and Clayton Nottleman for so energetically being my emissaries at the Provincetown Bookshop, and to Miladinka Milic for Sydney's amazing cover designs. And to Kyre Song, who is so much more than my web guy.

To my wonderful patrons: Chip Capelli, Mark Cortale, Michael Ponestowski, Freddy Biddle, Margo Nash, Amanda Robinson, Ann Robinson, Susan Blood, and Sydnia Czarnecki. I couldn't do what I do without you.

Special thanks to Pat Medina for rescuing me from the worst of my plot holes and setting me on the path to the Monument.

Thanks to Erin Andrews for the eagle-eyed editing. Any mistakes that remain here are mine, not hers. And to the New England chapter of the Sisters in Crime, for keeping me engaged with other writers.

Come to Carnival: there usually aren't any explosions, and it's the biggest and best party ever!

About the Author

Award-winning author Jeannette de Beauvoir writes mystery and historical fiction that's been translated into 12 languages.

A Book Sense Book-of-the-Year finalist, she's a member of the Authors Guild, the Mystery Writers of America, Sisters in Crime, and the National Writers Union.

All her novels are firmly rooted in a sense of place, and her delight is to find characters true to the spaces in which they live. She herself lives and writes in a cottage in Provincetown, on Cape Cod, Massachusetts, and loves the collection of people who assemble at a place like land's end.

Find out more—and read her blog—at jeannettedebeauvoir.com

Did You Enjoy This Book?

If you did, please…

- **share your opinion** on Goodreads and/or Amazon;
- **visit my Amazon page** and check out some of my other books;
- give the book a boost by **telling people** about it on Facebook and Twitter;
- **subscribe to my newsletter** or **write to me** at jeannettedebeauvoir.com;
- ask your local bookseller **to stock** *A Killer Carnival;*
- make it your **choice for your next book club** meeting (I'll even join you by Skype or Zoom if you'd like me to!);
- **join my subscription site** at patre-on.com/jeannettedebeauvoir for exclusive content and glimpses of works in progress;
- and **watch for *The Christmas Corpses***, next in the Sydney Riley mystery series from Homeport Press!